'A brilliant, wonderful book . . . best of all is the humour'
Sunday Telegraph

'An exhilarating switchback swirl through different but interconnecting versions of the same two days, one in the Nineties and one in 1941'
Times Educational Supplement

'The third in this series explodes onto the book-shelves . . . side-splittingly funny'
Young Telegraph

'The stretches of imagination are breathtaking . . . The opportunities for Forties-versus-Nineties culture clash are milked for maximum farce'
Daily Mail

'Terry Pratchett's storytelling skills are exceptional . . . A brilliant story full of Pratchett's quirky and delightful humour'
The Bookseller

'Genuinely hilarious dialogue, fast plot: Pratchett remains the very best-known cure for bookphobics everywhere'
Mail on Sunday

★ Also available on audio cassette
† Also available as a Graphic Novel
‡ Also available as a Playtext

TERRY PRATCHETT

JOHNNY and the BOMB

CORGI BOOKS

JOHNNY AND THE BOMB
A CORGI BOOK : 0 552 52968 0

First published in Great Britain by Doubleday,
a division of Transworld publishers Ltd

PRINTING HISTORY
Doubleday edition published 1996
Corgi edition published 1997
Corgi edition reprinted 1997, 1998

Corgi Books are published by Transworld Publishers Ltd,
61–63 Uxbridge Road, London W5 5SA,
in Australia by Transworld Publishers (Australia) Pty Ltd,
15–25 Helles Avenue, Moorebank, NSW 2170,
and in New Zealand by Transworld Publishers (NZ) Ltd,
3 William Pickering Drive, Albany, Auckland.

Typeset in 12/13pt Monotype Bembo by
Phoenix Typesetting, Ilkley, West Yorkshire

Printed and bound in Great Britain by
Cox & Wyman Ltd, Reading, Berkshire.

I would like to thank the Meteorological Office, the Royal Mint and my old friend Bernard Pearson – who, if he doesn't know something, always knows a man who does – for their help in the research for this book. When historical details are wrong, it's my fault for not listening. But who knows what really happened in the other leg of the Trousers of Time?

Chapter 1

After the Bombs

It was nine o'clock in the evening, in Blackbury High Street.

It was dark, with occasional light from the full moon behind streamers of worn-out cloud. The wind was from the south-west and there had been another thunderstorm, which freshened the air and made the cobbles slippery.

A policeman moved, very slowly and sedately, along the street.

Here and there, if someone was very close, they might have seen the faintest line of light around a blacked-out window. From within came the quiet sounds of people living their lives – the muffled notes of a piano as someone practised scales, over and over again, and the murmur and occasional burst of laughter from the wireless.

Some of the shop windows had sandbags piled in front of them. A poster outside one shop urged people to Dig For Victory, as if it were some kind of turnip.

On the horizon, in the direction of Slate, the thin beams of searchlights tried to pry bombers out of the clouds.

The policeman turned the corner, and walked

up the next street, his boots seeming very loud in the stillness.

The beat took him up as far as the Methodist chapel, and in theory would then take him down Paradise Street, but it didn't do that tonight because there was no Paradise Street any more. Not since last night.

There was a lorry parked by the chapel. Light leaked out from the tarpaulin that covered the back.

He banged on it.

'You can't park that 'ere, gents,' he said. 'I fine you one mug of tea and we shall say no more about it, eh?'

The tarpaulin was pushed back and a soldier jumped out. There was a brief vision of the interior – a warm tent of orange light, with a few soldiers sitting around a little stove, and the air thick with cigarette smoke.

The soldier grinned.

'Gi'us a mug and a wad for the sergeant,' he said, to someone in the lorry.

A tin mug of scalding black tea and a brick-thick sandwich were handed out.

'Much obliged,' said the policeman, taking them. He leaned against the lorry.

'How's it going, then?' he said. 'Haven't heard a bang.'

'It's a 25-pounder,' said the soldier. 'Went right down through the cellar floor. You lot took a real pounding last night, eh? Want a look?'

'Is it safe?'

''Course not,' said the soldier cheerfully. 'That's why we're here, right? Come on.' He pinched out his cigarette and put it behind his ear.

'I thought you lot'd be guarding it,' said the policeman.

'It's two in the morning and it's been pissing down,' said the soldier. 'Who's going to steal an unexploded bomb?'

'Yes, but . . . ' The sergeant looked in the direction of the ruined street.

There was the sound of bricks sliding.

'Someone is, by the sound of it,' he said.

'What? We've got warning signs up!' said the soldier. 'We only knocked off for a brew-up! Oi!'

Their boots crunched on the rubble that had been strewn across the road.

'It *is* safe, isn't it?' said the sergeant.

'Not if someone drops a dirty great heap of bricks on it, no! Oi! You!'

The moon came out from behind the clouds. They could make out a figure at the other end of what remained of the street, near the wall of the pickle factory.

The sergeant skidded to a halt.

'Oh, no,' he whispered. 'It's Mrs Tachyon.'

The soldier stared at the small figure that was dragging some sort of cart through the rubble.

'Who's she?'

'Let's just take it quietly, shall we?' said the policeman, grabbing his arm.

He shone his torch and set his face into a sort of mad friendly grin.

'That you, Mrs Tachyon?' he said. 'It's me, Sergeant Bourke. Bit chilly to be out at this time of night, eh? Got a nice warm cell back at the station, yes? I daresay there could be a big hot mug of cocoa for you if you just come along with me, how about that?'

'Can't she read all them warning signs? Is she mental?' said the soldier, under his breath. 'She's right by the house with the bomb in the cellar!'

'Yes . . . no . . . she's just different,' said the sergeant. 'Bit . . . touched.' He raised his voice. 'You just stay where you are, love, and we'll come and get you. Don't want you hurting yourself on all this junk, do we?'

'Here, has she been looting?' said the soldier. 'She could get shot for that, pinching stuff from bombed-out houses!'

'No-one's going to shoot Mrs Tachyon,' said the sergeant. 'We *know* her, see? She was in the cells the other night.'

'What'd she done?'

'Nothing. We let her kip in a spare cell in the station if it's a nippy night. I gave her a tanner and pair of ole boots what belong to me mum only yesterday. Well, look at her. She's old enough to be your granny, poor old biddy.'

Mrs Tachyon stood and watched them owlishly as they walked, very cautiously, towards her.

The soldier saw a wizened little woman wearing

what looked like a party dress with layers of other clothes on top, and a woolly hat with a bobble on it. She was pushing a wire cart on wheels. It had a metal label on it.

'Tes-co,' he said. 'What's that?'

'Dunno where she gets half her stuff,' muttered the sergeant.

The trolley seemed to be full of black bags. But there were other things, which glittered in the moonlight.

'I know where she got *that* stuff,' muttered the soldier. 'That's been pinched from the pickle factory!'

'Oh, half the town was in there this morning,' said the sergeant. 'A few jars of gherkins won't hurt.'

'Yeah, but you can't have this sort of thing. 'Ere, you! Missus! You just let me have a look at—'

He reached towards the trolley.

Some sort of demon, all teeth and glowing eyes, erupted from it and clawed the skin off the back of his hand.

'Blast! 'Ere, help me get hold of—'

But the sergeant had backed away.

'That's Guilty, that is,' he said. 'I should come away if I was you!'

Mrs Tachyon cackled.

'Thunderbirds Are Go!' she chortled. 'Wot, no bananas? That's what *you* think, my old dollypot!'

She hauled the trolley round and trotted off, dragging it behind her.

'Hey, don't go in *there*—' the soldier shouted.

The old woman hauled the trolley over a pile of bricks. A piece of wall collapsed behind her.

The last brick hit something far below, which went *boink*.

The soldier and the policeman froze in mid-run.

The moon went behind a cloud again.

In the darkness, there was a ticking sound. It was far off, and a bit muffled, but in that pool of silence both men heard it all the way up their spines.

The sergeant's foot, which had been in the air, came down slowly.

'How long've you got if it starts to tick?' he whispered.

There was no-one there. The soldier was accelerating away.

The policeman ran after him and was halfway up the ruins of Paradise Street before the world behind him suddenly became full of excitement.

It was nine o'clock in the evening, in Blackbury High Street.

In the window of the electrical shop, nine TVs showed the same picture. Nine televisions projected their flickering screens at the empty air.

A newspaper blew along the deserted pavement until it wrapped around the stalks in an ornamental flowerbed. The wind caught an empty lager tin and bowled it across the pavement until it hit a drain.

The High Street was what Blackbury District Council called a Pedestrian Precinct and Amenity

Area, although no-one was quite sure what the amenities were, or even what an amenity *was*. Perhaps it was the benches, cunningly designed so that people wouldn't sit on them for too long and make the place untidy. Or maybe it was the flower-beds, which sprouted a regular crop of the hardy perennial Crisp Packet. It couldn't have been the ornamental trees. They'd looked quite big and leafy on the original drawings a few years ago, but what with cutbacks and one thing and another, no-one had actually got around to planting any.

The sodium lights made the night cold as ice.

The newspaper blew on again, and wrapped itself around a yellow litter bin in the shape of a fat dog with its mouth open.

Something landed in an alleyway and groaned.

'Tick tick tick! Tickety Boo! Ow! National . . . Health . . . Service . . . '

The interesting thing about worrying about things, thought Johnny Maxwell, was the way there was always something new to worry about.

His friend Kirsty said it was because he was a natural worrier, but that was because she didn't worry about *anything*. She got angry instead, and did things about it, whatever *it* was. He really envied the way she decided what *it* was and knew exactly what to do about *it* almost instantly. Currently she was saving the planet most evenings, and foxes at weekends.

Johnny just worried. Usually they were the same

old worries – school, money, whether you could get AIDS from watching television, and so on. But occasionally one would come out of nowhere like a Christmas Number One and knock all the others down a whole division.

Right now, it was his mind.

'It's not exactly the same as being ill,' said Yo-less, who'd read all the way through his mother's medical encyclopedia.

'It's not being ill at all. If lots of bad things have happened to you it's healthy to be depressed,' said Johnny. 'That's sense, isn't it? What with the business going down the drain, and Dad pushing off, and Mum just sitting around smoking all the time and everything. I mean, going around smiling and saying, "Oh, it's not so bad" – that *would* be mental.'

'That's right,' said Yo-less, who'd read a bit about psychology as well.

'My gran went mental,' said Bigmac. 'She— ow!'

'Sorry,' said Yo-less. 'I wasn't looking where I put my foot but, fair's fair, you weren't either.'

'It's just dreams,' said Johnny. 'It's nothing *mad*.'

Although, he had to admit, it was dreams during the day, too. Dreams so real that they filled his eyes and ears.

The planes . . .

The bombs . . .

And the fossil fly. Why that? There'd be these nightmares, and in the middle of it, there'd be the fly. It was a tiny one, in a piece of amber. He'd saved up for it and done a science project on it. But it wasn't even scary-looking. It was just a fly from millions of years ago. Why was *that* in a nightmare?

Huh. *School teachers?* Why couldn't they be like they were supposed to be and just chuck things at you if you weren't paying attention? Instead they all seemed to have been worrying about him and sending notes home and getting him to see a specialist, although the specialist wasn't too bad and at least it got him out of Maths.

One of the notes had said he was 'disturbed'. Well, who wasn't disturbed? He hadn't shown it to his mum. Things were bad enough as it was.

'You getting on all right at your grandad's?' said Yo-less.

'It's not too bad. Grandad does the housework most of the time anyway. He's good at fried bread. And Surprise Surprise.'

'What's that?'

'You know that stall on the market that sells tins that've got the labels off?'

'Yes?'

'Well, he buys loads of those. And you've got to eat them once they're opened.'

'Yuk.'

'Oh, pineapple and meatballs isn't too bad.'

They walked on through the evening street.

The thing about all of us, Johnny thought, the *sad* thing is that we're not very good. Actually that's not the worst part. The worst part is we're not even much good at being not much good.

Take Yo-less. When you looked at Yo-less you might think he had possibilities. He was black. Technically. But he never said 'Yo', and only said 'check it out' in the supermarket, and the only person he ever called a mother was his mother. Yo-less said it was racial stereotyping to say all black kids acted like that but, however you looked at it, Yo-less had been born with a defective cool. *Trainspotters* were cooler than Yo-less. If you gave Yo-less a baseball cap he'd put it on the right way round. That's how, well, *yo-less* Yo-less was. Sometimes he actually wore a tie.

Now, Bigmac . . . Bigmac *was* good. He was good at Maths. Sort of. It made the teachers wild. You could show Bigmac some sort of horrible equation and he'd say 'x=2.75' and he'd be right. But he never knew *why*. 'It's just what it is,' he'd say. And that was *no* good. Knowing the answers wasn't what Maths was about. Maths was about showing how you worked them out, even if you got them wrong. Bigmac was also a skinhead. Bigmac and Bazza and Skazz were the last three skinheads in Blackbury. At least, the last three who weren't someone's dad. And he had LOVE and HAT on his knuckles, but only in Biro because when he'd gone to get tattooed he fainted. And he bred tropical fish.

As for Wobbler . . . Wobbler wasn't even a nerd. He *wanted* to be a nerd but they wouldn't let him join. He had a Nerd Pride badge and he messed around with computers. What Wobbler wanted was to be a kid in milk-bottle-bottom glasses and a deformed anorak, who could write amazing software and be a millionaire by the time he was twenty, but he'd probably settle for just being someone whose computer didn't keep smelling of burning plastic every time he touched it.

And as for Johnny . . .

. . . if you go mad, do you know you've gone mad? If you don't, how do you know you're *not* mad?

'It wasn't a bad film,' Wobbler was saying. They'd been to Screen W at the Blackbury Odeon. They generally went to see any film that promised to have laser beams in it somewhere.

'But you can't travel in time without messing things up,' said Yo-less.

'That's the whole point,' said Bigmac. 'That's what you *want* to do. I wouldn't mind joining the police if they were *time* police. You'd go back and say, "Hey, are you Adolf Hitler?" and when he said, "Achtung, that's me, ja" . . . *Kablooeee!* With the pump-action shotgun. End of problem.'

'Yes, but supposing you accidentally shot your own grandfather,' said Yo-less patiently.

'I wouldn't. He doesn't look a bit like Adolf Hitler.'

'Anyway, you're not that good a shot,' said Wobbler. 'You got kicked out of the Paintball Club, didn't you?'

'Only 'cos they were jealous that they hadn't

thought of a paintball hand grenade before I showed them how.'

'It was a *tin* of *paint*, Bigmac. A two-litre tin.'

'Well, yeah, but in *contex'* it was a hand grenade.'

'They said you might at least have loosened the lid a bit. Sean Stevens needed stitches.'

'I didn't mean *actually* shooting your *actual* grand-father,' said Yo-less, loudly. 'I mean messing things up so maybe you're not actually born or your time machine never gets invented. Like in that film where the robot is sent back to kill the mother of the boy who's going to beat the robots when he grows up.'

'Good one, that,' said Bigmac, strafing the silent shops with an invisible machine gun.

'But if he never got born how did they know he'd existed?' said Yo-less. 'Didn't make any sense to me.'

'How come you're such an expert?' said Wobbler.

'Well, I've got three shelves of Star Trek videos,' said Yo-less.

'Anorak alert!'

'Nerd!'

'Trainspotter!'

'*Anyway*,' said Yo-less, 'if you changed things, maybe you'd end up not going back in time, and there you would be, back in time, I mean, except you never went in the first place, so you wouldn't be able to come back on account of not having gone. *Or*, even if you could get back, you'd get back to another time, like a sort of parallel dimension, because if the thing you changed hadn't happened then you wouldn't've gone, so you could only come back to somewhere you never went. And there you'd be – stuck.'

They tried to work this out.

'Huh, you'd have to be mad even to understand time travel,' said Wobbler eventually.

'Job opportunity for you there, Johnny,' said Bigmac.

'*Bigmac*,' said Yo-less, in a warning voice.

'It's all right,' said Johnny. 'The doctor said I just worry about things too much.'

'What kind of loony tests did you have?' said Bigmac. 'Big needles and electric shocks and that?'

'No, Bigmac,' sighed Johnny. 'They don't do that. They just ask you questions.'

'What, like "are you a loony?"'

'It'd be sound to go a *long* way back in time,' said Wobbler. 'Back to the dinosaurs. No chance of killing your grandad then, unless he's *really* old. Dinosaurs'd be all right.'

'Great!' said Bigmac. 'Then I could wipe 'em out with my plasma rifle! Oh, yes!'

'Yeah,' said Wobbler, rolling his eyes. 'That'd explain a lot. Why did the dinosaurs die out sixty-five million years ago? Because Bigmac couldn't get there any earlier.'

'But you haven't *got* a plasma rifle,' said Johnny.

'If Wobbler can have a time machine, then I can have a plasma rifle.'

'Oh, all right.'

'And a rocket launcher.'

A time machine, thought Johnny. That *would* be something. You could get your life exactly as you wanted it. If something nasty turned up, you could just go back and make sure that it didn't. You could go wherever you wanted and nothing bad would ever have to happen.

Around him, the boys' conversation, as their conversations did, took on its own peculiar style.

'Anyway, no-one's proved the dinosaurs *did* die out.'

'Oh, yeah, right, sure, they're still around, are they?'

'I mean p'raps they only come out at night, or are camouflaged or something . . .'

'A brick-finished stegosaurus? A bright red Number 9 brontosaurus?'

'Hey, neat idea. They'd go round pretending to be a bus, right, and people could get on – but they wouldn't get off again. Oooo-Eee-Oooo . . .'

'Nah. False noses. False noses and beards. Then just when people aren't expecting it – UNK! Nothing on the pavement but a pair of shoes and a really big bloke in a mac, shuffling away . . .'

Paradise Street, thought Johnny. Paradise Street was on his mind a lot, these days. Especially at night.

I bet if you asked the people *there* if time travel was a good idea they'd say yes. I mean, no-one knows what happened to the dinosaurs, but we know what happened to Paradise Street.

I wish I could go back to Paradise Street.

Something hissed.

They looked around. There was an alleyway between the charity clothes shop and the video library. The hissing came from there, except now it had changed into a snarl.

It wasn't at all pleasant. It went right into his ears and right through Johnny's modern brain and right down into the memories built into his very bones. When an early ape had cautiously got down out of its tree and wobbled awkwardly along the ground, trying out this new 'standing upright' idea all the younger apes were talking about, this was exactly the kind of snarl it hated to hear.

It said to every muscle in the body: run away and climb something. And possibly throw down some coconuts, too.

'There's something in the alley,' said Wobbler, looking around in case there were any trees handy.

'A werewolf?' said Bigmac.

Wobbler stopped. 'Why should it be a werewolf?' he said.

'I saw this film, *Curse of the Revenge of the Werewolf*,' said Bigmac, 'and someone heard a snarl like that and went into a dark alley, and next thing, he was lying there with all his special effects spilling out on the pavement.'

'Huh,' quavered Wobbler. 'There's no such things as werewolves.'

'You go and tell it, then.'

Johnny stepped forward.

There was a shopping trolley lying on its side just inside the alley, but that wasn't unusual. Herds of shopping trolleys roamed the streets of Blackbury. While he'd never seen one actually moving, he sometimes suspected that they trundled off as soon as his back was turned.

Bulging carrier bags and black plastic dustbin liners lay around it, and there was a number of jars. One of them had broken open, and there was a smell of vinegar.

One of the bundles was wearing trainers.

You didn't see that very often.

A terrible monster pulled itself over the top of the trolley and spat at Johnny.

It was white, but with bits of brown and black as well. It was scrawny. It had three and a half legs but only one ear. Its face was a mask of absolute, determined evil. Its teeth were jagged and yellow, its breath as nasty as a pepper spray.

Johnny knew it well. So did practically everyone else in Blackbury.

'Hello, Guilty,' he said, taking care to keep his hands by his sides.

If Guilty was here, and the shopping trolley was here . . .

He looked down at the bundle with the trainers.

'I think something's happened to Mrs Tachyon,' he said.

The others hurried up.

It only looked like a bundle, because Mrs

Tachyon tended to wear everything she owned, all at once. This was a woolly hat, about twelve jerseys and a pink ra-ra skirt, then bare pipe-cleaner legs down to several pairs of football socks and the huge trainers.

'Is that *blood*?' said Wobbler.

'Ur,' said Bigmac. 'Yuk.'

'I think she's alive,' said Johnny. 'I'm sure I heard a groan.'

'Er . . . I know first aid,' said Yo-less, uncertainly. 'Kiss of life and stuff.'

'Kiss of life? *Mrs Tachyon?* Yuk,' said Bigmac.

Yo-less looked very worried. What seemed simple when you did it in a nice warm hall with the instructor watching seemed a lot more complicated in an alleyway, especially with all the woolly jumpers involved. Whoever invented first aid hadn't had Mrs Tachyon in mind.

Yo-less knelt down gingerly. He patted Mrs Tachyon vaguely, and something fell out of one of her many pockets. It was fish and chips, wrapped in a piece of newspaper.

'She's always eating chips,' said Bigmac. 'My brother says she picks thrown-away papers out of the bin to see if there's any chips still in 'em. Yuk.'

'Er . . . ' said Yo-less desperately, as he tried to find a way of administering first aid without actually touching anything.

Finally Johnny came to his rescue and said, 'I know how to dial 999.'

Yo-less sagged with relief. 'Yes, yes, that's right,' he said. 'I'm pretty sure you mustn't move people, on account of breaking bones.'

'Or the crust,' said Wobbler.

Chapter 2

Mrs Tachyon

Mrs Tachyon had always been there, as long as Johnny could remember. She was a bag lady before people knew what bag ladies were, although strictly speaking she was a trolley woman.

It wasn't a *normal* supermarket trolley, either. It looked bigger, the wires looked thicker. And it hurt like mad when Mrs Tachyon pushed it into the small of your back, which she did quite a lot. It wasn't that she did it out of nastiness – well, it *probably* wasn't – but other people just didn't exist on Planet Tachyon.

Fortunately, one wheel squeaked. And if you didn't get accustomed to moving away quickly when you heard the *squee . . . squee . . . squee* coming, the monologue was another warning.

Mrs Tachyon talked all the time. You could never be quite certain who she was talking to.

' . . . I sez, that's what you sez, is it? That's what *you* think. An' I could get both hands in yer mouth and still wind wool, I sez. Oh, yes. Tell Sid! Yer so skinny yer can close one eye and yer'd look like a needle, I sez. Oh, yes. They done me out of it! Tell that to the boys in khaki! That's a pelter or I don't know what is!'

But quite often it was just a mumble, with occasional triumphant shouts of 'I *told* 'em!' and 'That's what *you* think!'

The trolley with its squeaky wheel could turn up behind you at any hour of the day or night. No-one knew when to expect it. Nor did anyone know what was in all those bags. Mrs Tachyon tended to rummage a lot, in bins and things. So no-one wanted to find out.

Sometimes she'd disappear for weeks on end. No-one knew where she went. Then, just when everyone was beginning to relax, there'd be the *squee . . . squee . . . squee* behind them and the stabbing pain in the small of the back.

Mrs Tachyon picked things out of the gutter. That was probably how she'd acquired Guilty, with his fur like carpet underlay, broken teeth, and boomerang-shaped backbone. When Guilty walked, which wasn't often since he preferred to ride in the trolley, he tended to go around in circles. When he ran, usually because he was trying to fight something, the fact that he only had one and a half legs in front meant that sooner or later his back legs would overtake him, and by then he was always in such a rage that he'd bite his own tail.

Even DSS, the rabid dog owned by Syd the Crusty, which once ate a police Alsatian, would run away at the sight of Guilty spinning towards him, frantically biting himself.

★　　★　　★

The ambulance drove off, blue light flashing.

Guilty watched Johnny from the trolley, going cross-eyed with hatred.

'The ambulance man said she looked as if she'd been hit by something,' said Wobbler, who was also watching the cat. It was never a good idea to take your eye off Guilty.

'What're we going to do with all this stuff?' said Johnny.

'Yeah, can't leave it,' said Bigmac. 'That'd be littering.'

'But it's her stuff,' said Johnny.

'Don't look at *me*,' said Bigmac. 'Some of those bags *squelch*.'

'And there's the cat,' said Johnny.

'Yeah, we ought to kill the cat,' said Bigmac. 'It took all the skin off my hand last week.'

Johnny cautiously pulled the trolley upright. Guilty clung to it, hissing.

'He likes you,' said Bigmac.

'How can you tell?'

'You've still got both eyes.'

'You could take it along to the RSPCA in the morning,' said Yo-less.

'I suppose so,' said Johnny, 'but what about the trolley? We can't just leave it here.'

'Yeah, let's push it off the top of the multistorey,' said Bigmac.

Johnny prodded a bag. It moved a bit, and then flowed back, with an unpleasant oozing noise.

'Y'know, my brother said Mrs Tachyon killed

her husband years ago and then went mental and they never found his body,' said Bigmac.

They looked at the bags.

'None of them is big enough for a dead body,' said Yo-less, who wasn't allowed to watch horror movies.

'Not a *whole* one, no,' said Bigmac.

Yo-less took a step back.

'*I* heard she stuck his head in the oven,' said Wobbler. 'Very messy.'

'Messy?' said Yo-less.

'It was a microwave oven. Get it? If you put a—'

'Shut up,' said Yo-less.

'I heard she's really, really rich,' said Bigmac.

'Stinking rich,' said Wobbler.

'Look, I'll just . . . I'll just put in it in my grandad's garage,' said Johnny.

'I don't see why we have to do it,' said Yo-less. 'There's supposed to be Care in the Community or something.'

'He doesn't keep much in there now. And then in the morning . . . '

Oh, well. The morning was another day.

'And while you've got it you could have a rummage to see if there's any money,' said Bigmac.

Johnny glanced at Guilty, who snarled.

'No, I like a hand with all its fingers on,' he said. 'You lot come with me. I'd feel a right clod pushing this by myself.'

The fourth wheel squeaked and bounced as

he pushed the trolley down the street.

'Looks heavy,' said Yo-less.

There was a snigger from beside him.

'Well, they say *Mr* Tachyon was a very big man—'

'Just shut up, Bigmac.'

It's me, he thought, as the procession went down the street. It's like on the Lottery, only it's the *opposite*. There's this big finger in the sky and it comes through your window and flicks you on the ear and says 'It's YOU – har har har'. And you get up and think you're going to have a normal day and suddenly you're in charge of a trolley with one squeaky wheel and an insane cat.

'Here,' said Wobbler. 'These fish and chips are still warm.'

'What?' said Johnny. 'You picked up her actual fish and chips?'

Wobbler backed away. 'Well, yeah, why not, shame to let them go to waste—'

'They might have got her spit on 'em,' said Bigmac. 'Yuk.'

'They haven't even been unwrapped, actually,' said Wobbler, but he did stop unwrapping them.

'Put them in the trolley, Wobbler,' said Johnny.

'Dunno who wraps fish and chips in newspaper round here,' said Wobbler, tossing the package onto the pile in the trolley. 'Hong Kong Henry doesn't. Where'd she get them?'

★   ★   ★

Sir John was normally awakened at half past eight every morning by a butler who brought him his breakfast, another butler who brought him his clothes, a third butler whose job it was to feed Adolf and Stalin if necessary, and a fourth butler who was basically a spare.

At nine o'clock his secretary came and read him his appointments for today.

When he did so this morning, though, he found him still staring at his plate with a strange expression. Adolf and Stalin swam contentedly in the tank by his desk.

'Five different kinds of pill, some biscuits made of cardboard and a glass of orange juice with all the excitement removed,' said Sir John. 'What's the point of being the richest man in the world – I am still the richest man in the world, aren't I?'

'Yes, Sir John.'

'Well, what's the point if it all boils down to pills for breakfast?' He drummed his fingers on the table. 'Well . . . I've had enough, d'y'hear? Tell Hickson to get the car out.'

'Which car, Sir John?'

'The Bentley.'

'Which Bentley, Sir John?'

'Oh, one I haven't used lately. He can choose. And find Blackbury on the map. We own a burger bar there, don't we?'

'Er . . . I think so, Sir John. Wasn't that the one where you personally chose the site? You said you just knew it would be a good one. Er . . . but today you've got appointments to see the chairman of—'

'Cancel 'em all. I'm going to Blackbury. Don't tell

'em I'm coming. Call it . . . a lightning inspection. The secret of success in business is to pay attention to the little details, am I right? People get underdone burgers or the fries turn out to be too soggy and before you know where you are the entire business is down around your ears.'

'Er . . . if you say so, Sir John.'

'Right. I'll be ready in twenty minutes.'

'Er . . . you could, perhaps, leave it until tomorrow? Only the committee did ask that—'

'No!' The old man slapped the table. 'It's got to be today! Today's when it all happens, you see. Mrs Tachyon. The trolley. Johnny and the rest of them. It's got to be today. Otherwise . . . ' He pushed away the dull yet healthy breakfast. 'Otherwise it's this for the rest of my life.'

The secretary was used to Sir John's moods, and tried to lighten things a little.

'Blackbury . . . ' he said. 'That's where you were evacuated during the war, wasn't it? And you were the only person to escape when one of the streets got bombed?'

'Me and two goldfish called Adolf and Stalin. That's right. That's where it all started,' said Sir John, getting up and going over to the window. 'Go on, jump to it.'

The secretary didn't go straightaway. One of his jobs was to keep an eye on Sir John. The old boy was acting a bit odd, people had said. He'd taken to reading very old newspapers and books with words like 'Time' and 'Physics' in the title, and sometimes he even wrote angry letters to very important scientists. When you're the richest man in the world, people watch you very closely.

'Adolf and Stalin,' said Sir John, to the whole world

33

in general. 'Of course, these two are only their descend-
ants. It turned out that Adolf was female. Or was it
Stalin?'

Outside the window, the gardens stretched all the way
to some rolling hills that Sir John's landscape gardener had
imported specially.

'Blackbury,' said Sir John, staring at them. 'That's
where it all started. The whole thing. There was a boy
called Johnny Maxwell. And Mrs Tachyon. And a cat,
I think.'

He turned.

'Are you still here?'

'Sorry, Sir John,' said the secretary, backing out and
shutting the door behind him.

'That's where it all started,' said Sir John. 'And that's
where it's all going to end.'

Johnny always enjoyed those first few moments in
the morning before the day leapt out at him. His
head was peacefully full of flowers, clouds,
kittens—

His hand still *hurt*.

Horrible bits of last night rushed out from hiding
and bounced and gibbered in front of him.

There was a shopping trolley full of unspeakable
bags in the garage. There was also a spray of milk
across the wall and ceiling where Guilty had showed
what he thought of people who tried to give him
an unprovoked meal. Johnny had had to use the
biggest Elastoplast in the medicine tin afterwards.

He got up, dressed, and went downstairs. His

34

mother wouldn't be up yet and his grandad was definitely in the front room watching Saturday morning TV.

Johnny opened the garage door and stepped back hurriedly, in case a ball of maddened fur came spinning out.

Nothing happened.

The dreadful trolley stood in the middle of the floor. There was no sign of Guilty.

It was, Johnny thought, just like those scenes in films where you know the monster is in the room somewhere . . .

He jumped sideways, just in case Guilty was about to drop out of the ceiling.

It was bad enough seeing the wretched cat. *Not* seeing it was worse.

He scurried out and shut the door quickly, then went back into the house.

He probably ought to tell someone official. The trolley belonged to Mrs Tachyon (actually, it probably belonged to Mr Tesco or Mr Safeway) so it might be stealing if he kept it.

As he went back inside, the phone rang. There were two ways he could tell. Firstly, the phone rang. Then his grandfather shouted 'Phone!', because he never answered the phone if he thought there was a chance it could be answered by someone else.

Johnny picked it up.

'Can I speak to—' said Yo-less, in his Speaking to Parents voice.

'It's me, Yo-less,' said Johnny.

'Hey, you know Mrs Tachyon?'

'Of course I—'

'Well, my mum was on duty at the hospital last night. She's got horrible bruises and everything. Mrs Tachyon, I mean, not my mum. Someone really had a go at her, she said. My mum, not Mrs Tachyon. She said we ought to tell the police.'

'What for?'

'We might have seen something. Anyway . . . er . . . someone might think it was . . . us . . . '

'*Us?* But we called the ambulance!'

'*I* know that. Er . . . and you've got her stuff . . . '

'Well, we couldn't just leave it there!'

'*I* know that. But . . . well, we did have Bigmac with us . . . '

And that was it, really. It wasn't that Bigmac was actually *evil*. He'd happily fire imaginary nuclear missiles at people but he wouldn't hurt a fly, unless perhaps it was a real hard biker fly which'd given him serious grief. However, he did have a problem with cars, especially big fast ones with the keys still in the ignition. And he *was* a skinhead. His boots were so big that it was quite hard for him to fall over.

According to Sergeant Comely of Blackbury police station, Bigmac was guilty of every unsolved crime in the town, whereas in real life he was probably only guilty of ten per cent, maximum. He *looked* like trouble. No-one looking at Bigmac would think he was innocent of *anything*.

'And Wobbler, too,' Yo-less added.

And Wobbler would admit to anything if you got him frightened enough. All the great unsolved mysteries of the world – the Bermuda Triangle, the Marie Celeste, the Loch Ness Monster – could be sorted out in about half an hour if you leaned a bit on Wobbler.

'I'll go by myself, then,' said Johnny. 'Simpler that way.'

Yo-less sighed with relief. 'Thanks.'

The phone rang just as Johnny put it down again.

It started saying 'Hello? Hello?' before he got it to his ear.

'Er . . . hello?' he said.

'Is that *you*?' said a female voice. It wasn't exactly an unpleasant one, but it had a sharp, penetrating quality. It seemed to be saying that if you *weren't* you, then it was *your* fault. Johnny recognized it instantly. It was the voice of someone who dialled wrong numbers and then complained that the phone was answered by people she didn't want to speak to.

'Yes. Er . . . yes. Hello, Kirsty.'

'It's Kasandra, actually.'

'Oh. Right,' said Johnny. He'd have to make a note. Kirsty changed her name about as often as she changed her clothes, although at least these days she was sticking to ones beginning with K.

'Have you heard about old Mrs Tachyon?'

'I *think* so,' said Johnny, guardedly.

'Apparently a gang of yobs beat her up last night. She looked as though a bomb'd hit her. Hello? Hello? Hello?'

'I'm still here,' said Johnny. Someone had filled his stomach with ice.

'Don't you think that's shameful?'

'Er. Yes.'

'One of them was black.'

Johnny nodded dismally at the phone. Yo-less had explained about this sort of thing. He'd said that if one of his ancestors had joined Attila the Hun's huge horde of millions of barbarians and helped them raid Ancient Rome, people would've definitely remembered that one of them was black. And this was Yo-less, who collected brass bands, had a matchbox collection and was a known spod.

'Er,' he said, 'it was us. I mean, *we* didn't beat her up, but we found her. I got the ambulance and Yo-less tried— Yo-less was definitely *thinking* about first aid . . . '

'Didn't you tell the police?'

'No—'

'Honestly, I don't know what would happen if I wasn't around! You've got to tell them now. I'll meet you at the police station in half an hour. You know how to tell the time? The big hand is—'

'Yes,' said Johnny, miserably.

'It's only two stops on the bus from your house. You know about catching buses?'

'Yes, yes, yes, of course I—'

'You need money. That's the round stuff

38

you find in your pockets. *Ciao*.'

Actually, after he'd been to the toilet, he felt a bit better about it all. Kirs— Kasandra took charge of things. She was the most organized person Johnny knew. In fact she was so organized that she had too much organization for one person, and it over-flowed in every direction.

He was her friend. More or less, anyway. He wasn't sure he'd ever been given a choice in the matter. Kirs— *Kasandra* wasn't good at friends. She told him so herself. She'd said it was because of a character flaw, only because she was Ki— Kasandra, she thought it was a character flaw in everyone else.

The more she tried to help people by explaining to them how stupid they were, the more they just wandered off for no reason at all. The only reason Johnny hadn't was that he *knew* how stupid he was.

But sometimes – not often – when the light was right and she wasn't organizing anything, he'd look at Ki— Kasandra and wonder if there weren't two kinds of stupidity: the basic El Thicko kind that he had, and a highly specialized sort that you only got when you were stuffed too full of intelligence.

He'd better tell Grandad where he was going, he thought, just in case the power went off or the TV broke down and he wondered where Johnny had gone.

'I'm just off to—' he began, and then said, 'I'm just off out.'

'Right,' said Grandad, without taking his eyes off

the set. 'Hah! Look, there he goes! Right in the gunge tank!'

Nothing much was going on in the garage.

After a while, Guilty crawled out from his nest among the black plastic sacks and took up his usual position in the front of the cart, where he was wont to travel on the offchance that he could claw somebody.

A fly banged on the window pane for a while and then went back to sleep.

And the bags moved.

They moved like frogs in oil, slithering very slowly around each other. They made a rubbery, squeaky noise, like a clever conjurer trying to twist an animal out of balloons.

There were other noises, too. Guilty didn't pay them much attention because you couldn't attack noises and, besides, he was pretty well used to them by now.

They weren't very clear. They might have been snatches of music. They might have been voices. They might have been a radio left on, but slightly off station and two rooms away, or the distant roar of a crowd.

Johnny met Kasandra outside the police station.

'You're lucky I've got some spare time,' she said. 'Come on.'

Sergeant Comely was on the desk. He looked up as Johnny and Kasandra came in, then looked back at the book he was writing in, and then looked up again slowly.

'You?'

'Er, hello, Sergeant Comely,' said Johnny.

'What is it this time? Seen any aliens lately?'

'We've come about Mrs Tachyon, Sergeant,' said Kasandra.

'Oh yes?'

Kasandra turned to Johnny.

'Go on,' she said. 'Tell him.'

'Er . . . ' said Johnny. 'Well . . . me and Wobbler and Yo-less and Bigmac . . .'

'Wobbler and Yo-less and Bigmac and I,' said Kasandra.

Sergeant Comely looked at her.

'All five of you?' he said.

'I was just correcting his grammar,' said Kasandra.

'Do you do that a lot?' said the sergeant. He looked at Johnny. 'Does she do that a lot?'

'All the time,' said Johnny.

'Good grief. Well, go on. You, not her.'

When Sergeant Comely had been merely PC Comely he'd visited Johnny's school to show everyone how nice the police were, and had accidentally locked himself into his own handcuffs. He was also a member of the Blackbury Morris Men. Johnny had actually seen him wearing bells around his knees and waving two hankies in the air. These were important things to remember at a time like this.

'Well . . . we were proceeding along . . . ' he began.

'And no jokes.'

Twenty minutes later, they walked slowly down the steps of the police station.

'Well, that wasn't too bad,' said Kasandra. 'It's not as though you were arrested or anything. Have you really got her trolley?'

'Oh, yes.'

'I liked the look on his face when you said you'd bring Guilty in. He went quite pale, I thought.'

'What's next-of-kin mean? He said she'd got no next-of-kin.'

'Relatives,' said Kasandra. 'Basically, it means relatives.'

'None at all?'

'That isn't unusual.'

'Yes,' said Johnny, 'but generally there's a cousin in Australia you don't know about.'

'Is there?'

'Well, apparently *I've* got a cousin in Australia, and I didn't know about her till last month, so it can't be that unusual.'

'The state of Mrs Tachyon is a terrible Indictment on Society,' said Kasandra.

'What's indictment mean?'

'It means it's wrong.'

'That she's got no relatives? I don't think you can get them from the Governm—'

'No, that she's got no home and just wanders

around the place living on what she can find. Something Ought to be Done.'

'Well, I suppose we could go and see her,' said Johnny. 'She's only in St Mark's.'

'What good would that do?'

'Well, it might cheer *her* up a bit.'

'Do you know, you start almost every sentence with "Well"?'

'Well—'

'Going hospital visiting won't do anything about the disgusting neglect of street people and the mentally ill, will it?'

'Probably not. She just might be a bit cheered up, I suppose.'

Kasandra walked in silence for a moment.

'It's just that . . . I've got a thing about hospitals, if you must know. They're full of sick people.'

'We could take her something she likes. And she'd probably be glad to know that Guilty is OK.'

'They smell bad, too,' said Kasandra, not listening to him. 'That horrible disinfectant smell.'

'When you're up close to Mrs Tachyon you won't notice.'

'You're just going on about it because you know I hate hospitals, aren't you?'

'I . . . just think we ought to do it. Anyway, I thought you did things like this for your Duke of Edinburgh award or whatever it was.'

'Yes, but there was some *point* in that.'

'We could go towards the end of visiting time so

43

we won't be there very long. That's what everyone else does.'

'Oh, all *right*,' said Kasandra.

'We'd better take her something, too. You have to.'

'Like grapes, you mean?'

Johnny tried to picture Mrs Tachyon eating grapes. It didn't work. 'I'll think about it.'

The garage door swung back and forth, slowly.

Inside the garage there was:

A concrete floor. It was old and cracked and soaked in oil. Animal footprints crossed it, embedded in the concrete, suggesting that a dog had run across it when it was being laid. This happens in every patch of wet concrete, everywhere. There were also a couple of human footprints, fossilized in time, and now filled with black grease and dust. In other words, it was more or less like any piece of concrete. There was also:

A tool bench.

Most of a bicycle, upside down, and surrounded by tools and bits of bike in a haphazard manner which suggested that someone had mastered the art of taking a bike to bits without succeeding in the craft of putting it back together again.

A lawnmower entangled in a garden hosepipe, which is what always happens in garages, and isn't at all relevant.

A trolley, overflowing with plastic bags of all kinds, but most particularly six large black ones.

A small pile of jars of pickles, where Johnny had carefully stacked them last night.

The remains of some fish and chips. As far as Guilty was concerned, catfood only happened to other cats.

A pair of yellow eyes, watching intently from the shadows under the bench.

And that was all.

3

Bags of Time

To be honest about it, Johnny didn't much like hospitals either. Mostly, the people he'd gone to visit in them were not going to come out again. And no matter how they tried to cheer the place up with plants and pictures, it never looked friendly. After all, no-one was there because they wanted to be.

But Kirsty was good at finding out things and getting harassed people to give her answers, and it didn't take long to find Mrs Tachyon's ward.

'That's her, isn't it?' she said.

Kasandra pointed along the line of beds. One or two of them didn't have visitors around them, but there was no mistaking the one belonging to Mrs Tachyon.

She was sitting up in bed in a hospital night-gown and her woolly hat, over which she had a pair of hospital headphones.

Mrs Tachyon stared intently in front of her, and jigged happily among the pillows.

'She looks happy enough,' said Kasandra. 'What's she listening to?'

'I couldn't say for sure,' said the nurse. 'All I

know is the headphones aren't plugged in. Are you relatives?'

'No. We're—' Kasandra began.

'It's a sort of project,' said Johnny. 'You know . . . like weeding old people's gardens and that sort of thing.'

The nurse gave him an odd look, but the magic 'project' word did its usual helpful stuff.

She sniffed. 'Can I smell vinegar?' she said.

Kasandra glared at Johnny. He tried to look innocent.

'We've just brought some grapes,' he said, showing her the bag.

Mrs Tachyon didn't look up as they dragged chairs over to her bed.

Johnny had never spoken to her in his life, except to say 'sorry' when she rammed him with her trolley. He wasn't sure how to start now.

Kasandra leaned over and pulled one earphone aside.

'Hello, Mrs Tachyon!' she said

Mrs Tachyon stopped jigging. She turned a beady eye on Kasandra, and then on Johnny. She had a black eye, and her stained white hair looked frizzled at the front, but there was something horribly *unstoppable* about Mrs Tachyon.

'Indeed? That's what *you* think!' she said. 'Call again tomorrow, baker, and we'll take a crusty one! Poor old biddy, is it? That's what *you* think! Millennium hand and shrimp? Free teeth and corsets? Maybe, for them as likes it, but not me, thank you so much. Wot, no bananas? I had a house, oh yes, but it's all black men now. Hats.'

'Are they treating you all right?' said Kasandra.

'Don't you worry! Right as rain and twice as ninepence. Hah! Tick tick bang! I'd like to see them try. There's puddings. Of course, I remember when it was all fields, but would they listen?'

Kasandra looked at Johnny.

'I think she's a bit . . . confused,' she said. 'She doesn't understand anything I'm saying.'

'But we don't understand anything she's saying, either,' said Johnny, who felt confused all the time in any case.

Mrs Tachyon adjusted her headphones and started to boogie again.

'I don't believe this,' said Kasandra. 'Excuse *me*.'

She pulled the headphones off the woolly hat and listened to them.

'The nurse was right,' she said. 'There's nothing at all.'

Mrs Tachyon bounced up and down happily.

'One born every minute!' she chortled.

Then she winked at Johnny. It was a bright, knowing wink, from Planet Tachyon to Planet Johnny.

'We've brought you some grapes, Mrs Tachyon,' he said.

'That's what *you* think.'

'Grapes,' said Johnny firmly. He opened the

bag, exposing the steaming greaseproof fish and chip paper inside. Her eyes widened. A scrawny hand shot out from under the covers, grabbed the packet, and disappeared under the blanket again.

'Him and his coat,' she said.

'Don't mention it. Er. I'm keeping your trolley safe. And Guilty is all right, although I don't think he's eaten anything apart from some chips and my hand.'

'I blame Mr Chamberlain,' said Mrs Tachyon.

A bell tinkled.

'Oh dear that's the end of visiting time my word don't the hours just fly past what a shame,' said Kasandra, standing up quickly. 'Nice to have met you Mrs Tachyon sorry we have to be going come on Johnny.'

'Lady Muck,' said Mrs Tachyon.

She nodded at Johnny.

'What's the word on the street, mister man?'

Johnny tried to think like Mrs Tachyon.

'Er . . . "No Parking"?' he suggested.

'That's what *you* think. Them's bags of time, mister man. Mind me bike! Where your mind goes, the rest of you's bound to follow. Here today and gone yesterday! Doing it's the trick! Eh?'

Johnny stared. It was as though he had been listening to a lot of static on the radio and then, just for a second, there was this one clear signal.

The other Mrs Tachyon came back.

'He's mixing sugar with the sand, Mr McPhee!' she said. 'That's what *you* think.'

'What did you have to go and give her them for?' Kasandra hissed, as she strode out of the ward. 'She needs a proper healthy balanced diet! Not hot chips! What did you give her them for?'

'Well, I thought hot chips would be exactly what someone'd like who'd got used to cold chips. Anyway, she didn't get any supper last night. Hey, there was something very odd about—'

'She *is* very odd.'

'You don't like her much, do you?'

'Well, she didn't even say thank you.'

'But *I* thought she was an unfortunate victim of a repressive political system,' said Johnny. 'That's what you said when we were coming here.'

'Yes, all right, but courtesy doesn't cost anything, *actually*. Come on, let's get out of here.'

'Hello?' said someone behind them.

'They've found out about the chips,' muttered Kirsty, as she and Johnny turned around.

But it wasn't a nurse bearing down on them, unless the hospital had a plain clothes division.

It was a young woman in glasses and a worried hairstyle. She also had boots that would have impressed Bigmac, and a clipboard.

'Um . . . do you two *know* Mrs . . . er . . . Tachyon?' she said. 'Is that her name?'

'I suppose so,' said Johnny. 'I mean, that's what everyone calls her.'

'It's a very odd name,' said the woman. 'I suppose it's foreign.'

'We don't actually *know* her,' said Kasandra. 'We were just visiting her out of social concern.'

The woman looked at her. 'Good grief,' she said. She glanced at her clipboard.

'Do you know anything about her?' she said. 'Anything at all?'

'Like what?' said Johnny.

'Anything. Where she lives. Where she comes from. How old she is. Anything.'

'Not really,' said Johnny. 'She's just around. You know.'

'She must *sleep* somewhere.'

'Don't know.'

'There's no records of her *anywhere*. There's no records of *anyone* called Tachyon anywhere,' said the woman, her voice suggesting that this was a major criminal offence.

'Are you a social worker?' said Kasandra.

'Yes. I'm Ms Partridge.'

'I think I've seen you talking to Bigmac,' said Johnny.

'Bigmac? Who's Bigmac?'

'Er . . . Simon . . . Wrigley, I think.'

'Oh, yes,' said Ms Partridge darkly. 'Simon. The one who wanted to know how many cars he had to steal to get a free holiday in Africa.'

'And *he* said *you* said you'd only send him if cannibalism was still—'

'Yes, yes,' said Ms Partridge, hurriedly. When she'd started the job, less than a year ago, she'd firmly believed that everything that was wrong with the world was the fault of Big Business and the Government. She believed even more firmly now that it was all the fault of Bigmac.

'He was dead impressed, he said—'

'But you don't actually *know* anything about Mrs Tachyon, do you?' said the social worker. 'She had a trolley full of junk, but no-one seems to know where it is.'

'Actually—' Kasandra began.

'I don't know where it is either,' said Johnny firmly.

'It'd be very helpful if we could find it. It's amazing what they hoard,' said Ms Partridge. 'When I was in Bolton there was an old lady who'd saved every—'

'We'll miss the bus,' said Kasandra. 'Sorry we can't help, Miss Partridge. Come on, Johnny.'

She pulled him out of the building and down the steps.

'You *have* got the trolley, haven't you,' she said. 'You *told* me.'

'Yes, but I don't see why people should take it away from her or poke around in it. You wouldn't want people poking around in your stuff.'

'My mother said she was married to an airman

in the Second World War and he never came back and she went a bit strange.'

'My grandad said he and his friends used to tip up her trolley when *he* was a boy. He said they did it just to hear her swear.'

Kasandra hesitated.

'What? How old is your grandad?'

'Dunno. About sixty-five.'

'And how old is Mrs Tachyon, would you say?'

'It's hard to tell under all those wrinkles. Sixty?'

'Doesn't that strike you as odd?'

'What?'

'Are you dense or something? She's *younger* than your grandfather!'

'Oh . . . well . . . perhaps there was another Mrs Tachyon?'

'That isn't very likely, is it?'

'So you're saying she's a hundred years old?'

'Of course not. There's bound to be a sensible explanation. What's your grandfather's memory like?'

'He's good at television programmes. You'll be watching, and then he'll say something like, "Hey, him . . . the one in the suit . . . he was the police-man in that programme, *you* know, the one with the man with the curly hair, couple of years ago, *you* know." And if you buy anything, he can always tell you that you could get it for sixpence and still have change when he was a lad.'

'Everyone's grandad does that,' said Kasandra severely.

'Sorry.'

'Haven't you looked in the bags?'

'No . . . but she's got some odd stuff.'

'How do you mean?'

'Well . . . there are these jars of pickles . . . '

'Well? Old people like pickles.'

'Yes, but these are . . . kind of new and old at the same time. And there was fish and chips wrapped up in a newspaper.'

'Well?'

'No-one wraps up fish and chips in newspaper these days. But they all looked fresh. I had a look because I thought I might as well give the fish to the cat, and the newspaper . . . '

Johnny stopped.

What could he say? That he *knew* that front page? He knew every word of it. He'd found the same one on the microfiche in the library and the librarian had given him a copy to help him with his history project. He'd never seen it apart from the copy and the fuzzy image on the screen and suddenly there it was, unfolded in front of him, greasy and vinegary but undoubtedly . . .

. . . *new.*

'Well, let's have a *look* at them, at least. That can't hurt.'

Kasandra was like that. When all else failed, she tried being reasonable.

The big black car sped up the motorway. There were two motorcyclists in front and two more behind, and another

54

car trailing behind them containing some serious men in suits who listened to little radios a lot and wouldn't even trust their mothers.

Sir John sat by himself in the back of the black car, with his hands crossed on his silver-topped walking stick and his chin on his hands.

There were two screens in front of him, which showed him various facts and figures to do with his companies around the world, beamed down to him from a satellite, which he also owned. There were also two fax machines and three telephones.

Sir John sat and stared at them.

Then he reached over and pressed the button that operated the driver's intercom.

He'd never liked Hickson much. The man had a red neck. On the other hand, he was the only person there was to talk to right now.

'Do you believe it's possible to travel in time, Hickson?'

'Couldn't say, sir,' said the chauffeur, without turning his head.

'It's been done, you know.'

'If you say so, sir.'

'Time's been changed.'

'Yes, sir.'

'Of course, you wouldn't know about it, because you were in the time that it changed into.'

'Good thing for me then, sir.'

'Did you know that when you change time you get two futures heading off side by side?'

'Must have missed that in school, sir.'

'Like a pair of trousers.'

'Definitely something to think about, Sir John.'

Sir John stared at the back of the man's neck. It really was very red, and had unpleasant little patches of hair on it. He hadn't hired the man, of course. He had people who had people who had people who did things like that. It had never occurred to them to employ a chauffeur with an interest in something else besides what the car in front was doing.

'Take the next left turn,' he snapped.

'We're still twenty miles from Blackbury, sir.'

'Do what you're told! Right now!'

The car skidded, spun half around, and headed up the off-ramp with smoke coming from its tyres.

'Turn left!'

'But there's traffic coming, Sir John!'

'If they haven't got good brakes they shouldn't be on the road! Good! You see? Turn right!'

'That's just a lane! I'll lose my job, Sir John!'

Sir John sighed.

'Hickson, I'd like to lose all our little helpers. If you can get me to Blackbury by myself I will personally give you a million pounds. I'm serious.'

The chauffeur glanced at his mirror.

'Why didn't you say, sir? Hold on to something, sir!'

As the car plunged down between high hedges, all three of the telephones started to ring.

Sir John stared at them for a while. Then he pressed the button that wound down the nearest window and, one by one, threw them out.

The fax machine followed.

After some effort he managed to detach the two screens, and they went out too, exploding very satisfactorily when they hit the ground.

He felt a lot better for that.

4

Men in Black

The bus rumbled along the road towards Johnny's house.

'There's no sense in getting *excited* about Mrs Tachyon,' said Kasandra. 'If she's really been a bag lady here for years and years, then there's a whole range of perfectly acceptable explanations without having to resort to far-fetched ones.'

'What's an acceptable explanation?' said Johnny. He was still wrapped up in the puzzle of the newspaper.

'She's an alien, possibly.'

'That's acceptable?'

'Or she could be an Atlantean. From Atlantis. You know? The continent that sank under the sea thousands of years ago. The inhabitants were said to be very long-lived.'

'They could breathe underwater?'

'Don't be silly. They sailed away just before it sank, and built Stonehenge and the Pyramids and so on. They were scientifically very advanced, actually.'

Johnny looked at her with his mouth open. You expected this sort of thing from Bigmac and the others, but not from Ki— Kasandra, who was already doing A-levels at fourteen years old.

'I didn't know that,' he said.

'It was hushed up by the government.'

'Ah.' Kasandra was good at knowing things that were hushed up by the government, especially considering that they had been, well, hushed up. They were always slightly occult. When giant footprints had appeared around the town centre during some snow last year there had been two theories. There was Kir— Kasandra's, which was that it was Bigfoot, and Johnny's, which was that it was a combination of Bigmac and two 'Giant Rubber Feet, A Wow at Parties!!!!' from the Joke Emporium in Penny Street. Ki— Kasandra's theory had the backing of so many official sources in the books she'd read that it practically outweighed Johnny's, which was merely based on watching him do it.

Johnny thought about the Atlanteans, who'd all be two metres tall in Greek togas and golden hair, leaving the sinking continent in their amazing golden ships. And on the deck of one of them, Mrs Tachyon, ferociously wheeling her trolley.

Or you could imagine Attila the Hun's barbarians galloping across the plain and, in the middle of the line of horsemen, Mrs Tachyon on her trolley. Off her trolley, too.

'What happens,' said Kasandra, 'is that if you see a UFO or a yeti or something like that, you get a visit from the Men in Black. They drive around in big black cars and menace people who've seen strange things. They say they're working for the government but they're really working for the secret society that runs everything.'

'How d'you know all this?'

'Everyone knows. It's a well-known fact. I've been waiting for something like this, ever since the mysterious rain of fish we had in September,' said Kasandra.

'You mean, when there was that gas leak under the tropical fish shop?'

'Yes, we were *told* it was a leak under the tropical fish shop,' said Kasandra darkly.

'What? Of course it was the gas leak! They found the shopkeeper's wig in the telephone wires in the High Street! Everyone had guppies in their gutters!'

'The two might have been coincidentally connected,' said Kasandra reluctantly.

'And you still believe that those crop circles last year weren't made by Bigmac even though he swears they were?'

'All right, perhaps *some* of them might have been made by Bigmac, but who made the first ones, eh?'

'Bazza and Skazz, of course. They read about 'em in the paper and decided we should have some, too.'

'They didn't necessarily make *all* of them.'

Johnny sighed. As if life wasn't complicated enough, people had to set out to make it worse. It had been difficult enough before he'd heard about spontaneous combustion. You could be sitting peacefully in your chair, minding your own business, and next minute, *whoosh*, you were just a pair of shoes with smoke coming out. He'd taken to keeping a bucket of water in his bedroom for some weeks after reading about that.

And then there were all these programmes about aliens swooping down on people and taking them away for serious medical examinations in their flying saucers. If you were captured and taken away by aliens, but then they messed around with your brain so you forgot about them *and* they had time travel, so they could put you back exactly where you were before they'd taken you away . . . how would you know? It was a bit of a worry.

Kasandra seemed to think all this sort of thing was interesting, instead of some kind of a nuisance.

'Kasandra,' he said.

'Yes? What?'

'I wish you'd go back to Kirsty.'

'Horrible name. Sounds like someone who makes scones.'

' . . . I didn't mind Kimberly . . . '

'Hah! I now realize that was a name with "trainee hairdresser" written all over it.'

' . . . although Klymenystra was a bit over the top.'

'When was that?'

'About a fortnight ago.'

'I was probably feeling a bit gothy at the time.'

The bus pulled up at the end of Johnny's road, and they got off.

The garages were in a little cul-de-sac around the back of the houses. They weren't used much, at least for cars. Most of Grandad's neighbours parked in the street, so that they could enjoy complaining about stealing one another's parking spaces.

'You haven't even peeked in the bags?' said Kasandra, as Johnny fished in his pockets for the garage key.

'No. I mean, supposing they were full of old knickers or something?'

He pushed open the door.

The trolley was where he left it.

There was something odd about it that he couldn't quite put his finger on. It was clearly standing in the middle of the floor but managed to give the impression of moving very fast at the same time, as though it were a still frame from a movie.

Kasandra-formerly-Kirsty looked around.

'Bit of a dump,' she said. 'Why's that bike upside down over there?'

'It's mine,' said Johnny. 'It got a puncture yesterday. I haven't managed to repair it yet.'

Kasandra picked up one of the jars of pickle from the bench. The label was sooty. She wiped it and turned it towards the light.

'"Blackbury Preserves Ltd Gold-Medal Empire Brand Mustard Pickle",' she read. '"Six Premier Awards. Grand Prix de Foire Internationale des Conichons Nancy 1933. Festival of Pickles, Manchester, 1929. Danzig Pökelnfest 1928. Supreme Prize, Michigan State Fair, 1933. Gold Medal, Madras, 1931. Bonza Feed Award, Sydney, 1932. Made from the Finest Ingredients." And then there's a picture of some sort of crazed street kid jumping about, and it says underneath, "Up In The Air Leaps Little Tim, Blackbury Pickles Have Bitten Him." Very clever. Well, they're pickles. So what?'

'They're from the old pickle factory,' said Johnny. 'It got blown up during the war. At the same time as Paradise Street. Pickles haven't been made here for more than fifty years!'

'Oh, no!' said Kasandra. 'You don't mean . . . we're in a town where no pickles are made? That's creepy, that is.'

'You don't have to be sarcastic. It's just odd, was all I meant.'

Kasandra shook the jar. Then she picked up another sooty jar of gherkins, which sloshed as she turned it over.

'They've kept well, then,' she said.

'I tried one this morning,' said Johnny. 'It was nice and crunchy. And what about *this*?'

Out of his pocket came the newspaper that had wrapped Mrs Tachyon's fish and chips. He spread it out.

'It's an old newspaper,' said Johnny. 'I mean . . . it's very old, but not *old*. That's all stuff about the Second World War. But . . . it doesn't look old or feel old or smell old. It's . . .'

'Yes, I know, it's probably one of those reprinted newspapers you can get for the day you were born, my father got *me* one for—'

'Wrapping fish and chips?' said Johnny.

'It's odd, I must admit,' said Kasandra.

She turned and looked at him as though seeing him for the first time.

'I've waited *years* for something like this,' she said. 'Haven't you?'

'For something like Mrs Tachyon's trolley?'

'Try to pay attention, will you?'

'Sorry.'

'Haven't you ever wondered what'd happen if a flying saucer landed in your garden? Or you found some sort of magical item that let you travel in time? Or some old cave with a wizard that'd been asleep for a thousand years?'

'Well, as a matter of fact I *did* once find an old cave with—'

'I've read books and books about that sort of thing, and they're full of unintelligent children who go around saying "gosh". They just drift along having an *adventure*, for goodness' sake. They never seem to think of it as any kind of opportunity. They're never prepared. Well, I *am*.'

Johnny tried to imagine what'd happen if Kirsty was ever kidnapped by aliens. You'd probably end up with a galactic empire where everyone had sharp pencils and always carried a small torch in case of emergencies. Or they'd make a million robot copies who'd fly around the universe telling everyone not to be stupid and forcing them to be sensible.

'This is *obviously* something very odd,' she said. 'Possibly mystic. Possibly a time machine of some sort.'

And that was the thing about her. She arrived at an explanation. She didn't mess around with uncertainty.

'Didn't *you* think that?' she said.

'A time machine? A time shopping trolley?'

'Well, what other explanation fits the facts? Apart from possibly she was kidnapped by aliens and brought here at the speed of light, which is something they do a lot for some reason. But there might be something else, I'm sure you've thought of it.' She glanced at her watch. 'No hurry,' she added sarcastically. 'Take your time.'

'Well . . .'

'No rush.'

'Well . . . a time machine'd have flashing lights . . .'

'Why?'

'You've *got* to have flashing lights.'

'What for?'

Johnny wasn't going to give in.

'To flash,' he said.

'Really? Well, who says a time machine has to look like anything?' said Kasandra in a superior tone of voice, or at least an even more superior voice than the one she usually used. 'Or has to be powered by electricity?'

'Yo-less says you can't have time machines because everyone'd keep changing the future,' said Johnny.

'Oh? So what's the alternative? How come she turned up with this new old newspaper and all these new old pickle jars?'

'All right, but I don't go leaping to great big conclusions!'

In fact he did. He knew he did. All the time. But there was something about the way Kasandra argued that automatically made you take the other side.

He waved a hand at the trolley.

'I mean,' he said, 'do you really think something could just press the . . . oh, the handle, or the bags or something, and suddenly it's hello, Norman the Conqueror?'

He thumped his hand down on a black bag.

The world flashed in front of his eyes.

There was concrete under his feet, but there were no walls. At least, not much in the way of walls. They were one brick high.

A man cementing the new row looked up very slowly.

'Blimey,' he said, 'how did you get there?' Then he seemed to get a grip on himself. 'Hey, that concrete's still— Fred! You come here!'

A spaniel sitting by the man barked at Johnny and rushed forward, jumping up at Johnny and knocking him back against the trolley.

There was another flash. It was red and blue and it seemed to Johnny that he was squashed very flat and then pulled out again.

There were walls, and the shopping trolley was still in the middle of the floor, as was Kasandra, staring at him.

'You vanished for a moment,' she said, as if he'd done something wrong. 'What happened?'

'I . . . I don't know, how should I know?' said Johnny.

'Move your feet,' she said. 'Very slowly.'

He did. They met a very slight obstacle, a tiny ridge in the floor. He looked down.

'Oh, they're just the footprints in the cement,' he said. 'They've been . . . there . . . ages . . . '

Kasandra knelt down to look at the footprints he'd been standing in. They were ingrained with dust and dirt, but she made him take off his trainer and held it upside down by the print.

It matched exactly.

'See?' she said triumphantly. 'You're standing in your *own* footprints.'

Johnny stepped gingerly aside and looked at the footprints where he'd been standing. There was no doubt they'd been there a long time.

'Where did you go?'

'Back in time . . . I think. There was a man building this place, and a dog.'

'A dog,' said Kasandra. Her voice suggested that she would have seen something *much* more interesting. 'Oh, well. It's a start.'

She shifted the trolley. It was standing in four small grooves in the concrete. They were dirty and oily. They'd been there a long time, too.

'This,' said Kirsty, 'is no ordinary shopping trolley.'

'It's got Tesco written on it,' Johnny pointed out,

hopping up and down as he replaced his shoe. '*And a squeaky wheel.*'

'Obviously it's still switched on or something,' Kirsty went on, ignoring him.

'And that's time travel, is it?' said Johnny. 'I thought it'd be more exciting. You know – battles and monsters and things? And it's not much fun if all we can do is – *don't touch it!*'

Kasandra prodded a bag.

The air flickered and changed.

Kasandra looked around her. The garage hadn't changed in any way. Except—

'Who repaired your bike?' she said.

Johnny turned. His bike was no longer upside down with a wheel off, but leaning against the wall, both tyres quite full.

'You see, I notice things,' said Kasandra. 'I am remarkably observant. We must have gone into the future, when you've mended it.'

Johnny wasn't sure. He'd torn three inner tubes already, plus he'd also lost the thingy from the inside of the valve. Probably no time machine could ever go *so* far into the future that he'd be good at cycle repair.

'Let's have a look round,' said Kirsty. 'Obviously where we go is controlled by some factor I haven't discovered yet. If we're in the future, the important thing is to find out which horses are going to win races, and so on.'

'Why?'

'So we can bet money on them and become rich, of course.'

'I don't know how to bet!'

'One problem at a time.'

Johnny looked though the grimy window. The weather didn't look very different. There were no flying cars or other definite signs of futurosity. But Guilty was no longer under the bench.

'Grandad has a racing paper,' he said, feeling a bit light-headed.

'Let's go, then.'

'What? Into my house?'

'Of course.'

'Supposing I meet me?'

'Well, you've always been good at making friends.'

Reluctantly, Johnny led the way out of the garage. Garden paths in the future, he noted, were made of some gritty grey substance which was amazingly like cracked concrete. Back doors were an excitingly futuristic faded blue colour, with little dried flakes where the paint had bubbled up. It was locked, but his ancient key still fitted.

There was a rectangle on the floor consisting of spiky brown hairs. He wiped his feet on it, and looked at the time measurement module on the wall. It said ten past three.

The future was amazingly like the present.

'Now we've got to find a newspaper,' said Kirsty.

'It won't be a lot of help,' said Johnny. 'Grandad

keeps them around until he's got time to read them. They go back months. Anyway, everything's *normal*. This doesn't look very futuristic to *me*.'

'Don't you even have a calendar?'

'Yes. There's one on my bedside clock. I just hope I'm at school, that's all.'

According to the clock, it was the third of October.

'The day before yesterday,' said Johnny. 'Mind you, it could be the clock. It doesn't work very well.'

'Yuk. You *sleep* in here?' said Kirsty, looking around with an expression like a vegetarian in a sausage factory.

'Yes. It's my room.'

Kirsty ran her hand over his desk, which was fairly crowded at the moment.

'What're all these photocopies and photos and things?'

'*That's* the project I'm doing in History. We're doing the Second World War. So I'm doing Blackbury in the war.'

He tried to get between her and the desk, but Kirsty was always interested in things people didn't want her to see.

'Hey, this is you, isn't it?' she said, grabbing a sepia photograph. 'Since when did *you* wear a uniform and a pudding-basin haircut?'

Johnny tried to grab it. 'And that's Grandad when he was a bit older than me,' he mumbled. 'I tried to get him to talk about the war like the

70

teacher said but he tells me to shut up about it.'

'You're so *local*, aren't you,' said Kirsty. 'I can't imagine much happening here—'

'Something did happen,' said Johnny. He pulled out Mrs Tachyon's chip paper and jabbed at the front page with his finger. 'At 11.07pm on May 21, 1941. Bombs! Real bombs! They called it the Blackbury Blitz. And this is the paper from the day after. Look.' He rummaged among the stuff on his desk and pulled out a photocopy. 'See? I got a copy of the same page out of the library! But *this* paper's real, it's new!'

'If she *is* . . . from the past . . . why does she wear an old ra-ra skirt and trainers?' said Kirsty.

Johnny glared angrily at her. She had no *right* not to care about Paradise Street!

'Nineteen people got killed! In one night!' he said. 'There wasn't any warning! The only bombs that fell on Blackbury in the whole of the war! The only survivors were two goldfish in a bowl! It got blown into a tree and still had water in it! All the people got killed!'

Kirsty picked up a felt-tipped pen, but it didn't write because it had dried up. Johnny had a world-class collection of pens that didn't work.

She had this infuriating habit of appearing not to notice him when he was excited about something.

'You know you've still got Thomas the Tank Engine on your wallpaper?' she said.

'*What?* Have I? Gosh, I hadn't realized,' said Johnny, with what he hoped was sarcasm.

71

'It's OK to have Thomas the Tank Engine when you're seven, and it's quite cool to have it when you're nineteen, but it's not cool at thirteen. Honestly, if I wasn't here to help from time to time, you just wouldn't have a clue.'

'Grandad put it up a couple of years ago,' said Johnny. 'This was my room when I stayed with them. You know grandparents. It's Thomas the Tank Engine until you die.'

Then there was the click of the front door opening.

'Your grandad?' hissed Kirsty.

'He always goes shopping in town on Thursdays!' whispered Johnny. 'And Mum's at work!'

'Who else has got a key?'

'Only me!'

Someone started to climb the stairs.

'But I can't meet *me*!' said Johnny. 'I'd remember, wouldn't I? Yo-less says if you meet yourself the whole universe explodes! I'd remember that happening!'

Kirsty picked up the bedside lamp, and glanced at the design on it.

'Good grief, the Mr Men, you've still got Mr—'

'Shutupshutupshutup. What're you going to *do* with it?'

'Don't worry, you won't feel a thing, I learned how to do this in self-defence classes—'

The doorhandle turned. The door opened a fraction.

Downstairs, the phone rang.

The handle clicked back. Footsteps went downstairs again.

Johnny heard the phone picked up. A distant voice said: 'Oh, hi, Wobbler.'

Kirsty looked at Johnny and raised her eyebrows.

'Wobbler phoned,' said Johnny. 'About going to the movies yest— tomorrow. I just remembered.'

'Were you on the phone long?'

'Don't . . . think so. And I went to get a sandwich afterwards.'

'Where's your phone?'

'In the front room.'

'Let's go, then!'

Kirsty opened the door and darted down the stairs, with Johnny trailing behind her.

His coat was on the coat rack. He was *also* wearing it. He stood and stared.

'Come *on*,' hissed Kirsty.

She was almost at the bottom when the door started to open.

Johnny opened his mouth to say: oh, yes, I remember, I had to go and get my wallet to see if I'd got any money.

He desperately wanted not to meet himself. If the entire universe exploded, people would be bound to blame him afterwards . . .

. . . and there was a flash in front of his eyes.

The black car slid surreptitiously out of a side road just before a sign indicating that it was about to enter

BLACKBURY *(twinned with Aix-et-Pains)*.

'Nearly there, Sir John.'

'Good. What time are we in?'

'Er . . . quarter past eleven, sir.'

'That wasn't what I meant. If time was a pair of trousers, what leg would we be in?'

It occurred to Hickson the chauffeur that this might be quite a difficult million pounds to earn.

'They all got mixed up today, you see,' said a voice from the seat behind him.

'Right, sir. If I see any trousers, sir, you just tell me what leg to drive down.'

5

The Truth is Out of Here

Johnny was still on the stairs. Kirsty was still in front of him. The door was shut. His coat wasn't on the coat rack. The Blackbury Shopper, which was delivered on Fridays and stayed on the hall table until someone threw it away, was indeed on the table.

'We've time travelled again, haven't we,' said Kirsty, calmly. 'I think we're back to where we started. Possibly . . .'

'I saw the back of my own head!' whispered Johnny. 'My actual own back of my own head! Without mirrors or anything! No-one's ever done that since the Spanish Inquisition! How can you be so calm about this?'

'I'm just acting calm,' said Kirsty. 'This is even worse wallpaper, isn't it? Looks like an Indian restaurant.'

She opened the front door, and slammed it again.

'You know I said that if you started getting too interested in mysterious occult things these men in black cars turn up?'

'Yes? Well?'

'Look through the letterbox, will you?'

Johnny levered it open with a finger.

There was a car pulling up outside. It was black. Utterly. Black. Black tyres, black wheels, black headlights. Even the windows were darker than a pair of Mafia sunglasses. Here and there were bits of chrome, but they only made the blackness blacker by comparison.

It stopped. Johnny could just make out the shadow of the driver behind the tinted glass.

''S . . . just . . . coincidence,' he said.

'Your grandad often gets visitors like this, does he?' Kasandra demanded.

'Well . . . ' He didn't. Someone came round on Thursday to collect his football pools coupon and that was about it. Grandad was not one for the social whirl.

The car door opened. A man got out. He was wearing a black chauffeur's uniform. The car door shut. It shut with the kind of final, heavy *thonk* that only the most expensive car doors can achieve, because they are lined with money.

Johnny let go of the letterbox and jumped back.

A few seconds later, someone banged heavily on the door.

'Run!' whispered Kasandra

'Where?'

'The back door? Come *on*!'

'We haven't done anything wrong!'

'How do you know?'

Kasandra opened the back door and hurried down the path and into the garage, dragging

Johnny behind her. The trolley was still in the middle of the floor.

'Get ready to open the big doors and don't stop for anything!'

'Why?'

'Open the doors now!'

Johnny opened them, because practically anything was better than arguing with Kirsty.

The little garage area was empty, except for someone washing their car.

Johnny was nearly knocked aside as the trolley rattled out, with Kasandra pushing determinedly on the handle. It rattled across the concrete and lurched uncertainly into the alleyway that led to the next road.

'Didn't you see that programme about the flying saucer that crashed and these mysterious men turned up and hushed it all up?' said Kasandra.

'No!'

'Well, did you even *hear* about the flying saucer crashing?'

'No!'

'See?'

'All right, but in that case how come there was a TV programme about it, then?'

A car edged around the corner into the road.

'I can't waste time answering silly questions,' said Kasandra. 'Come *on*.'

She shoved the trolley as hard as she could. It rolled down the sloping pavement, the squeaky wheel bouncing and juddering over the slabs.

The car turned the corner very slowly, as though driven by someone who didn't know the area very well.

Johnny caught up with Kir-Kasandra and clung to the handle because the trolley was rocking all over the pavement.

The trolley, under its heavy load, began to pick up speed.

'Try to hold it back!'

'*I'm* trying! Are *you*?'

Johnny risked a look behind. The car seemed to be catching up.

He jumped onto the trolley.

'What are you playing at?' said Kirsty, who was far too worried to remember any new names now.

'Come on!'

He grabbed her hand and pulled her up on the other side of the cart. Now she was no longer holding the handle, it surged forward.

'Do you think this is *really* a time machine?' he said, as the rushing wind made the bags flutter.

'It must be!'

'D'you see that film where the car travelled in time when it went at eighty-eight miles an hour?'

They looked down. The wheels were screaming. Smoke was coming out of the axles. They looked up the hill. The car was catching them up. They looked down the hill. There were the traffic lights. The Blackbury by-pass was a solid wall of thundering traffic.

Then they looked up into each other's frightened faces.

'The lights are red! The lights are red! I don't want to die!' said Kirsty. 'I haven't even been to university!'

One hundred metres ahead, sixteen-wheeled lorries barrelled onwards, taking a million English razor blades from Sheffield to Italy and, coming the other way, a million Italian razor blades from Rome to England.

The trolley was, without a shadow of a doubt, going to smash right into the middle of them.

The air flickered.

And there were no lorries, or, rather, there *were* lorries, snorting and hissing and waiting at the lights. The lights ahead of Johnny were green.

The trolley rolled through, wheels screaming. Johnny looked up into the puzzled faces of the drivers.

Then he risked a look behind.

The black car had vanished.

There were no other turnings off the hill. Wherever it had gone, it hadn't got there by any means known to normal cars.

He met Kirsty's eyes.

'Where did it go?' she said. 'And what happened with the lights? Did we travel in time again?'

'You're wearing your mac!' said Johnny. 'You *were* wearing your old coat but now you're wearing your mac! Something's changed!'

She looked down, and then back up at him.

Beside the crossroads was the Neil Armstrong Shopping Mall. Johnny pointed to it.

'We can make this go into the car park!' he shouted.

The big black Bentley jerked to a halt at the side of the road.

'*They just vanished!' said Hickson, staring over the top of the wheel. 'That wasn't . . . this time travel stuff, was it? I mean, they just vanished!'*

'*I think they went from one* now *to another* now,' *said Sir John.*

'*Is that . . . like . . . these trousers you were going on about, sir?'*

'*I suppose you could say they went from one knee to the other. One 1996 to another 1996.'*

Hickson turned around in his seat.

'*Are* you *serious, sir? I saw this scientist on TV . . . you know, the one in the wheelchair . . . and there was all this stuff about other universes all crammed in, and—'*

'*He'd know the proper way of talking about it,' said Sir John. 'For the rest of us, it's easier to think about trousers.'*

'*What shall we do now, sir?'*

'*Oh, I think we wait until they come back to our* now.'

'*How long's that going to be?'*

'*About two seconds, I think . . .*'

* * *

In the shopping mall, a joke was going wrong.

'Make me . . . er,' said Bigmac, 'make me one with pickle and onion rings and fries.'

'Make me one with extra salad and fries, please,' said Yo-less.

Wobbler took a long look at the girl in the cardboard hat.

'Make me one with everything,' he said. 'Because . . . I'm going to become a Muslim!'

Bigmac and Yo-less exchanged glances.

'Buddhist,' said Yo-less, patiently. 'It's *Buddhist*! Make me one with everything because I'm going to become a Buddhist! It's Buddhists that want to be one with everything. Singing "om" and all that. You mucked it up! You were practising all the way down here and you still mucked it up!'

'Buddhists wouldn't have the burger,' said the girl. 'They'd have the Jumbo Beanburger. Or just fries and a salad.'

They stared at her.

'Vegetarianism,' said the girl. 'I may have to wear a paper hat but I haven't got a cardboard brain, thank you.' She glared at Wobbler. 'You want a bun with everything. You want fries with that?'

'Er . . . yes.'

'There you go. Have a day.'

The boys took their burgers and wandered back out into the mall.

'We do this every Saturday,' said Bigmac.

'Yes,' said Wobbler.

'And every Saturday we work out a joke.'

'Yes.'

'And you always mess up the punchline.'

'Well . . . it's something to do.'

And there wasn't much else to do at the mall. Sometimes there were displays and things. At Christmas there'd been a nice tableau of reindeer and Dolls of Many Countries that really moved (jerkily) to music, but Bigmac had found out where the controls were and speeded up everything four times, and a Norwegian's head had gone through the window of the cookie shop on the second floor.

All there was today in the way of entertainment were the people selling plastic window frames and someone else trying to get people to try a new artificial baked potato mix.

The boys sat down by the ornamental pond, and watched out for the security guards. You could always tell where Bigmac was in the mall by watching the flow of the security guards, several of whom had been hit by bits of disintegrating Scandinavian and bore a grudge. As far as anyone knew, Bigmac had never been guilty of anything other than the occasional confused approach to the ownership of other people's cars, but he had an amazing way of looking as though he was thinking about committing some rather daft crime, probably with a can of spray paint. His camouflage jacket didn't help. It might have worked in a jungle, but it tended to stand out when the background was the Olde Card and Cookie Shoppe.

'Old Johnny may be a bit of a nerd but it's always interesting when he's around,' said Wobbler. 'Stuff happens.'

'Yeah, but he hangs around with Kimberly or Kirsty or whoever she is today and she gives me the creeps,' said Yo-less. 'She's weird. She always looks at me as if I haven't answered a question properly.'

'Her brother told me everyone expects her to go to university next year,' said Bigmac.

Yo-less shrugged. 'You don't have to be dumb to be weird,' he said. 'If you're brainy you can be even weirder. It's all that intelligence looking for something to do. That's what I think.'

'Well, Johnny's weird,' said Bigmac. 'Well, he is. It's amazing the stuff that goes on in his head. Maybe he *is* a bit mental.'

'It's amazing the stuff that goes on *outside* his head,' said Wobbler. 'He's just—'

There was a crash somewhere in the mall, and people started to shout.

A shopping trolley rolled at high speed up the aisle, with shoppers running to get out of the way. It had a plastic window frame hanging on the front and was splashed with artificial potato. Johnny and Kirsty were hanging on either side.

He waved at them as he drifted past.

'Help us get this out of the back door!'

'That's old Mrs Tachyon's trolley, isn't it?' said Yo-less.

'Who cares?' said Bigmac. He put his burger down on the edge of the pond, where it was surreptitiously picked up by Wobbler, and ran after the trolley.

'Someone's chasing us,' Johnny panted, as they caught up.

'Brilliant!' said Bigmac. 'Who?'

'Some people in a big black car,' said Johnny. 'Only . . . they've vanished . . . '

'Oh, an *invisible* big black car,' said Yo-less.

'I see *them* all the time,' said Bigmac.

'Are you going to stand around all *day*?' Kirsty demanded. 'It's probably got some kind of special shield! Come *on*!'

The trolley wasn't massively heavy, although the piles of bags did weigh it down. But it did need a lot of steering. Even with all of them helping – or, Johnny thought later, perhaps *because* of all of them helping – it skidded and wobbled as they tried to keep it in a straight line.

'If we can get out of the other doors, we're in the High Street,' said Johnny. 'And it can't go in there because there's bollards and things.'

'I wish I had my five-megawatt laser cannon,' said Bigmac, as they fought the trolley round a corner.

'You haven't got a laser cannon,' said Yo-less.

'I know, that's why I wish I had one.'

'Ow!'

Wobbler leapt back.

'It bit me!' he screamed.

Guilty stuck his head out of the heap of bags and hissed at Johnny.

Security guards were strolling towards them. There were five kids arguing around a trolley, Bigmac was among them and, as Yo-less would have pointed out, one of them was black. This sort of thing attracts attention.

'This trolley might be a time machine,' said Johnny. 'And that car . . . Kirsty thinks someone's after it. I mean me. I mean us.'

'Great, how do we make it work?' said Bigmac.

'A time machine,' said Yo-less. 'Ah. Yes?'

'Where's this invisible car got to?' said Wobbler.

'We can't go out of the other doors,' said Kirsty, flatly. 'There's a couple of guards there.'

Johnny stared at the black dustbin liners. Then he picked one up and undid the string. For a moment his fingers felt cold and the air was full of faint whispers—

The mall vanished.

It vanished above them, and around them.

And below them.

They landed in a heap on the grass, about a metre below where they'd been standing. The trolley landed on top of them, one wheel slamming into the small of Johnny's back. Bags bounced out, and Guilty took the opportunity to scratch Bigmac's ear.

And then there was silence, except for Bigmac swearing.

Johnny opened his eyes. The ground sloped up all around him. There were low bushes at the top.

'If I asked what happened,' said Yo-less, from somewhere under Bigmac, 'what'd you say?'

'I *think* we may have travelled in time,' said Johnny.

'D'you get an electric feeling?' said Wobbler, clutching his jaw. 'Like . . . all your teeth standing on end?'

'Which way did we go?' said Yo-less, still talking in his deliberate voice. 'Are we talking dinosaurs, or mutant robots? I want to know this before I open my eyes.'

Kirsty groaned.

'Oh dear, it's going to be *that* kind of adventure after all,' she hissed, sitting up. 'It's just the sort of thing I didn't want to happen. Me, and four token boys. Oh, dear. Oh, dear. It's only a mercy we haven't got a dog.' She sat up and brushed some grass off her coat. 'Anyone got the least idea of where we are?'

'Ah,' said Yo-less. 'I see there's grass. That means no dinosaurs. I saw that in a film. Grass didn't evolve until after there were dinosaurs.'

Johnny stood up. His head was aching. He walked to the edge of the little hollow they'd landed in, and looked out.

'Really. Someone's been paying attention,' said

Kirsty. 'Well, that narrows it down to some time in the last sixty million years.'

'*Proper* time travellers have proper digital read-outs,' Wobbler grumbled. 'No grass? What did dinosaurs eat, then?'

'You only get digital time machine clocks in America,' said Bigmac. 'I saw a film about a time machine in Victorian England and it just had light bulbs. They ate other dinosaurs, didn't they?'

'You're not allowed to call them dinosaurs any more,' said Yo-less. 'It's speciesist. You have to call them pre-petroleum persons.'

'Yeah,' said Bigmac. 'One Million Years PC. Get it? 'Cos there was this film called One Million Years *BC*, but—'

Kirsty's mouth was open.

'Do you lot go on like this all the time?' she said. 'Yes, you do. I've noticed it before, actually. Rather than face up to facts, you start yakking on about weird things. When *are* we?'

'May the twenty-first,' said Johnny, sitting down next to her. 'Just gone half past three.'

'Oh yes?' said Kirsty. 'And how come you're so sure?'

'I went and asked a man who was walking his dog,' said Johnny.

'Did he say what year?'

Johnny met Kirsty's gaze. 'No,' he said. 'But I *know* what year.'

They climbed out of the hollow and pushed their way through the bushes.

A scrubby field stretched away below them. There were some allotment gardens at the bottom end of the field, and then a river, and then the town of Blackbury.

It was definitely Blackbury. There was the familiar rubber boot factory chimney. There were a few other tall chimneys as well. He'd never seen those before. The man with the dog was watching them from some way off. So was the dog. Neither of them seemed particularly Jurassic, although the dog looked somewhat suspicious.

'Wha . . ?' said Wobbler. 'Here, what's been happening? What have you done?'

'I told you we'd travelled in time,' said Kirsty. 'Weren't you listening?'

'I thought it was just some trick! I thought you were just messing about!' He gave Johnny a very worried look. 'This *is* just messing about, isn't it?'

'Yes.'

Wobbler relaxed.

'It's messing about with time travel,' said Johnny.

Wobbler looked scared again.

'Sorry. But that's Blackbury all right. It's just smaller. I think we're where the mall is *going* to be.'

'How do we get back?' said Yo-less.

'It just sort of happens, I think.'

'You're just doing it with hallucinations, aren't you,' said Wobbler, never a boy to let go of hope. 'It's probably the smell from the trolley. We'll come round in a minute and have a headache and it'll all be all right.'

'It just sort of happens?' said Yo-less. He was using his careful voice again, the voice that said there was something nasty on his mind. 'How do you get back?'

'There's a flash, and there you are,' said Kirsty.

'And you're back where you left?'

'Of course not. Only if you didn't move. Otherwise you go back to wherever where you are now is going to be then.'

There was silence while they all worked this out.

'You mean,' said Bigmac, 'that if you walk a couple of metres, you'll be a couple of metres away from where you started when you get back?'

'Yes.'

'Even if there's been something *built* there?' said Yo-less.

'Yes . . . no . . . I don't know.'

'So,' said Yo-less, still speaking very slowly, 'if there's a lot of concrete, what happens?'

They all looked at Kirsty. She looked at Johnny.

'I don't know,' he said. 'Probably you kind of . . . get lumped together.'

'Yuk,' said Bigmac.

There was a wail from Wobbler. Sometimes, when it involved something horrible, his mind worked very fast.

'I don't want to end up with just my arms sticking out of a concrete wall!'

'Oh, I don't think it'd happen like that,' said Yo-less.

Wobbler relaxed, but not much. 'How *would* it happen, then?' he said.

'What I *think* would happen is, see, all the atoms in your body, right, and all the atoms in the wall would be trying to be in the same place at the same time and they'd all smash together suddenly and—'

'And what?' said Kirsty.

'—and . . . er . . . bang, good night, Europe,' said Yo-less. 'You can't argue with nuclear physics, sorry.'

'My arms *wouldn't* end up sticking out of a wall?' said Wobbler, who hadn't quite caught up.

'No,' said Yo-less.

'Not a wall near here, anyway,' said Bigmac, grinning.

'Don't wind him up,' said Yo-less severely. 'This is serious. It could happen to *any* of us. We dropped when we landed, right? Does that mean that if we suddenly go back now we'll be sticking out of the floor of the mall, causing an instant atomic explosion?'

'They make enough fuss when you drop a Coke tin,' said Johnny.

'Where's Wobbler gone?' said Kirsty.

Wobbler was a disappearing shape, heading for the allotments. He shouted something.

'What'd he say?' she said.

'He said "I'm off home!"' said Johnny.

'Yeah, but,' said Bigmac, ' . . . where he's running now . . . if we're where the mall is . . . *will* be . . . then over there's the shopping estate. That field he's running across.' He squinted. 'That's where Currys is going to be.'

'How will we know we're about to go back?' said Yo-less.

'There's a sort of flicker for a moment,' said Johnny. 'Then . . . zap. Er . . . what'll happen if he comes out where there's a fridge or something? Is that as bad as a concrete wall?'

'I don't know much about fridge atoms,' said Yo-less. 'They might not be as bad as concrete atoms. But I shouldn't think anyone around here would need new wallpaper ever again.'

'Wow! An atomic Wobbler!' said Bigmac.

'Let's get the trolley and go after him,' said Johnny.

'We don't need it. Leave it here,' said Kirsty.

'No. It's Mrs Tachyon's.'

'There's just one thing I don't understand,' said Yo-less, as they hauled the trolley across the field.

'There's *millions* of things *I* don't understand,' said Johnny.

'What? *What?* What are you going on about now?'

'Televisions. Algebra. How skinless sausages hold together. Chinese,' said Johnny. 'I don't understand any of them.'

91

'The trolley's got no works,' said Yo-less. 'There's no time machinery.'

'Maybe the time is in the bags,' said Johnny.

'Oh, right! Bags of time? You can't just shove time in a bag!'

'Maybe Mrs Tachyon didn't know that. She's always picking up odds and ends of stuff.'

'You can't pick up time, *actually*. Time's what you pick things up *in*,' said Kirsty.

'My granny saves string,' said Bigmac, in the manner of someone who wants to make a contribution.

'Really? Well, you can't pick up the odd half-hour and knot it on to another ten minutes you've got spare, in case you haven't noticed,' said Kirsty. 'Honestly, don't they teach you any physics at your school? Fridge atoms was bad enough! What on earth's a fridge atom?'

'The smallest possible particle of fridge,' said Yo-less.

Perhaps you *could* save time, Johnny thought rebelliously. You could waste it, it could run through your fingers and you could put a stitch in it. Of course, perhaps that was only a manner of speaking and it all depended on how you looked at it, but Mrs Tachyon looked at things in a cork-screw kind of way.

He remembered touching a bag. Had time leaked out? *Something* had hissed through his fingers.

'You can't have the smallest possible particle of

fridge! It'd just be iron atoms and so on!'

'A fridge molecule, then. One atom of every-thing you need to make a fridge,' said Yo-less.

'You couldn't ha— well, all right, you *could* have one atom of everything you need to make a fridge but that wouldn't make it a fridge molecule because—' She rolled her eyes. 'What am I saying? You've got *me* thinking like that now!'

The rest of the universe said that time wasn't an object, it was just Nature's way of preventing everything from happening at once, and Mrs Tachyon had said: that's what *you* think . . .

The path across the field led through the allot-ments. They looked like allotments everywhere, with the occasional old man who looked exactly like the old men who worked on allotments. They wore the special old man's allotment trousers.

One by one, they stopped digging as the trolley bumped along the path. They turned and watched in a silent allotment way.

'It's probably Yo-less's coat they're looking at,' Kirsty hissed. 'Purple, green and yellow. It's plastic, right? Plastic hasn't been around for long. Of course, it might be Bigmac's *Heavy Mental* T-shirt.'

They're planting beans and hoeing potatoes, thought Johnny. And tonight there's going to be a crop of great big bomb craters . . .

'I can't see the by-pass,' said Bigmac. 'And there's no TV tower on Blackdown.'

'There's all those extra factory chimneys,

though,' said Yo-less. 'I don't remember any of those. And where's the traffic noise?'

It's May 21, 1941, thought Johnny. I *know* it.

There was a very narrow stone bridge over the river. Johnny stopped in the middle of it and looked back the way they'd come. A couple of the allotment men were still watching them. Beyond them was the sloping field they'd arrived in. It wasn't particularly pretty. It had that slightly grey tint that fields get when they're right next to a town and know that it's only a matter of time before they're under concrete.

'I remember when all this was buildings,' he said to himself.

'What're you going on about now?'

'Oh, nothing.'

'I recognize *some* of this,' said Bigmac. 'This is River Street. That's old Patel's shop on the corner, isn't it?'

But the sign over the window said: ★SMOKE WOODBINES★ J. Wilkinson (prop.).

'Woodbines?' said Bigmac.

'It's a kind of cigarette, obviously,' said Kirsty.

A car went past. It was black, but not the dire black of the one on the hill. It had mud and rust marks on it. It looked as though someone had started out with the idea of making a very large mobile jelly mould and had changed their mind about halfway through, when it was slightly too late. Johnny saw the driver crane his head to stare at them.

It was hard to tell much from the people on the streets. There were a lot of overcoats and hats, in a hundred shades of boredom.

'We shouldn't hang around,' said Kirsty. 'People are looking at us. Let's go and see if we can get a newspaper. I want to know when we are. It's so *gloomy*.'

'Perhaps it's the Depression,' said Johnny. 'My grandad's always going on about when he was growing up in the Depression.'

'No TV, everyone wearing old-fashioned clothes, no decent cars,' said Bigmac. 'No wonder everyone was depressed.'

'Oh, God,' said Kirsty. 'Look, try to be careful, will you? Any little thing you do could seriously affect the future. Understand?'

They entered the corner shop, leaving Bigmac outside to guard the trolley.

It was dark inside, and smelled of floorboards. Johnny had been on a school visit once, to a sort of theme park that showed you what things had been like in the all-purpose Olden Days. It had been quite interesting, although everyone had been careful not to show it, because if you weren't careful they'd sneak education up on you while your guard was down. The shop was a bit like that, only it had things the school one hadn't shown, like the cat asleep in the sack of dog biscuits. And the smell. It wasn't only floorboards in it. There was paraffin in it, and cooking, and candles.

A small lady in glasses looked at them carefully.

'Yes. What can I do for you?' she said. She nodded at Yo-less.

'Sambo's with you, dear, is he?' she added.

6

The Olden Days

Guilty lay on top of the bags and purred.

Bigmac watched the traffic. There wasn't a lot. A couple of women met one another as they were both crossing the street, and stood there chatting in the middle of the road, although occasionally one of them would turn to look at Bigmac.

He folded his arms over HEAVY MENTAL.

And then a car pulled up, right in front of him. The driver got out, glanced at Bigmac, and walked off down the street.

Bigmac stared at the car. He'd seen ones like it on television, normally in those costume dramas where one car and two women with a selection of different hats keep going up and down the same street to try to fool people that this isn't really the present day.

The keys were still in the ignition.

Bigmac wasn't a criminal, he was just around when crimes happened. This was because of stupidity. That is, *other people's* stupidity. Mainly other people's stupidity in designing cars that could go from 0–120mph in ten seconds and then selling them to even more stupid people who were only interested in dull things like fuel consumption and what colour the seats were. What was the point in that? That wasn't what a car was *for*.

The keys were still in the ignition.

As far as Bigmac was concerned, he was practically doing people a favour by really seeing what their cars could do, and no way was that stealing, because he always put the cars back if he could and they were often nearly the same shape. You'd think people'd be *proud* to know their car could do 130mph along the Blackbury by-pass instead of complaining all the time.

The keys were still in the ignition. There were a million places in the world where the keys could have been, but in the ignition was where they were.

Old cars like this probably couldn't go at any speed at all.

The keys were still in the ignition. Firmly, invitingly, in the ignition.

Bigmac shifted uncomfortably.

He was aware that there were people in the world who considered it wrong to take cars that didn't belong to them but, however you looked at it . . .

. . . the keys were still in the ignition.

Johnny heard Kirsty's indrawn breath. It sounded like Concorde taking off in reverse.

He felt the room grow bigger, rushing away on every side, with Yo-less all by himself in the middle of it.

Then Yo-less said, 'Yes, indeed. I'm with them. Lawdy, lawdy.'

The old lady looked surprised.

'My word, you speak English very well,' she said.

'I learned it from my grandfather,' said Yo-less, his voice as sharp as a knife. 'He ate only very educated missionaries.'

Sometimes Johnny's mind worked fast. Normally it worked so slowly that it embarrassed him, but just occasionally it had a burst of speed.

'He's a prince,' he said.

'Prince Sega,' said Yo-less.

'All the way from Nintendo,' said Johnny.

'He's here to buy a newspaper,' said Kirsty, who in some ways did not have a lot of imagination.

Johnny reached into his own pocket, and then hesitated.

'Only we haven't got any money,' he said.

'Yes we have, I've got a least two pou—' Kirsty began.

'We haven't got the *right* money,' said Johnny meaningfully. 'It was pounds and shillings and pence in those days, not pounds and pee—'

'Pee?' said the woman. She looked from one to the other like someone who hopes that it'll all make sense if they pay enough attention.

Johnny craned his head. There were a few newspapers still on the counter, even though it was the afternoon. One was *The Times*. He could just make out the date.

May 21, 1941.

'Oh, you have a paper, dear,' said the old woman, giving up, 'I don't suppose I shall sell any more today.'

'Thank you very much,' said Johnny, grabbing a paper and hurrying the other two out of the shop.

'Sambo,' said Yo-less, when they were outside.

'What?' said Kirsty. 'Oh, that. Never mind about that. Give me that newspaper.'

'My grandad came here in 1952,' said Yo-less, in the same plonking, hollow voice. 'He said little kids thought his colour'd come off if he washed.'

'Yes, well, I can see you're upset, but that's just how things were, it's all changed since then,' said Kirsty, turning the pages.

'*Then* hasn't even happened yet,' said Yo-less. 'I'm not stupid. I've read old books. We're back in golliwog history. Plucky niggers and hooray for the Empire. She called me *Sambo*.'

'Look,' said Kirsty, still reading the newspaper. 'This is the olden days. She didn't mean it . . . you know, nastily. It's just how she was brought up. You people can't expect us to rewrite history, you know.'

Johnny suddenly felt as though he'd stepped into a deep freeze. It was almost certainly the *you people*. Sambo had been an insult, but *you people* was worse, because it wasn't even personal.

He had never seen Yo-less so angry. It was a kind of rigid, brittle anger. How could someone as intelligent as Kirsty be so dumb? What she needed to do now was say something sensible.

'Well, I'm certainly glad you're here,' said Yo-less, sarcasm gleaming on his words. 'So's you can explain all this to me.'

'All right, don't go on about it,' she said, without looking up. 'It's not *that* important.'

It was amazing, Johnny thought. Kirsty had a sort of talent for striking matches in a firework factory.

Yo-less took a deep breath.

Johnny patted him on the arm.

'She didn't mean it . . . you know, nastily,' he said. 'It's just how she was brought up.'

Yo-less sagged, and nodded coldly.

'You know we're in the middle of a war, don't you,' said Kirsty. 'That's what we've ended up in. World War Two. It was very popular around this time.'

Johnny nodded.

May the twenty-first, 1941.

Not many people cared or even knew about it now. Just him, and the librarian at the public library who'd helped him find the stuff for the project, and a few old people. It was ancient history, after all. The olden days. And here he was.

And so was Paradise Street.

Until tonight.

'Are you all right?' said Yo-less.

He hadn't even known about it until he'd found the old newspapers in the library. It was – it was as if it hadn't *counted*. It had happened, but it wasn't a proper part of the war. And worse things had happened in a lot of other places. Nineteen people hardly mattered.

But he'd imagined it happening in *his* town. It was horribly easy.

The old men would go home from their allotments. The shops would shut. There wouldn't be many lights in any case, because of the blackout, but bit by bit the town would go to sleep.

And then, a few hours later, it'd happen.

It'd happen tonight.

Wobbler wheezed along the road. And he *did* wobble. It wasn't his fault he was fat, he'd always said, it was just his genetics. He had too many of them.

He was trying to run but most of the energy was getting lost in the wobbling.

He was trying to think, too, but it wasn't happening very clearly.

They hadn't gone time travelling! It was just a windup! They were always trying to wind him up! He'd get home and have a sit down, and it'd all be all right . . .

And this *was* home.

Sort of.

Everything was . . . smaller, somehow. The trees in the street were the wrong size and the cars were wrong. The houses looked . . . newer. And this was Gregory Road. He'd been along it millions of times. You went along halfway and turned into . . .

. . . into . . .

A man was clipping a hedge. He wore a high collar and tie *and* a pullover with a zig-zag pattern. He was also smoking a pipe. When he saw Wobbler he stopped clipping and took his pipe out of his mouth.

'Can I help you, son?' he said.

'I . . . er . . . I was looking for Seeley Crescent,' whispered Wobbler.

The man smiled.

'Well, I'm Councillor Edward Seeley,' he said, 'but I've never heard of a Seeley Crescent.' He called over his shoulder to a woman who was weeding a flowerbed. 'Have you heard of a Seeley Crescent, Mildred?'

'There's a big chestnut tree on the corner—' Wobbler began.

'We've got a chestnut tree,' said Mr Seeley, pointing to what looked like a stick with a couple of leaves on it. He smiled. 'It doesn't look much at the moment, but just you come back in fifty years' time, eh?'

Wobbler stared at it, and then at him.

It was a wide garden here, with a field beyond it. It struck him that it was quite wide enough for a road, if . . . one day . . . someone wanted to build a road . . .

'I will,' he said.

'Are you all right, young man?' said Mrs Seeley.

Wobbler realized that he wasn't panicking any more. He'd run out of panic. It was like being in a dream. *Afterwards*, it all sounded daft, but while you were in the dream you just got on with it.

It was like a rocket taking off. There was a lot of noise and worry and then you were in orbit, floating free, and able to look down on everything as if it weren't real.

It was an amazing feeling. Wobbler had spent a large part of his life being frightened of things, in a vague kind of way. There were always things he should have been doing, or shouldn't have done. But here it all didn't seem to matter. He wasn't even born yet – in a way, anyway – so absolutely nothing could be his fault.

'I'm fine,' he said. 'Thank you very much for asking. I'll . . . just be off back into town.'

He could feel them watching him as he wandered back down the road.

This *was* his home town. There were all sorts of clues that told him so. But all sorts of other things were . . . strange. There were more trees and fewer houses, more factory chimneys and fewer cars. A lot less colour, too. It didn't look much fun. He was pretty certain no-one here would even know what a pizza *was*—

''Ere, mister,' said a hoarse voice.

He looked down.

A boy was sitting by the side of the road.

It was almost certainly a boy. But its short trousers reached almost to its ankles, it had a pair of glasses with one lens blanked out with brown paper, its hair had been cut apparently with a lawnmower, and its nose was running. And its ears stuck out.

No-one had ever called Wobbler 'mister' before, except teachers when they wanted to be sarcastic.

'Yes?' he said.

'Which way's London?' said the boy. There was a cardboard suitcase next to him, held together with string.

Wobbler thought for a moment. 'Back that way,' he said, pointing. 'Dunno why there's no road signs.'

'Our Ron says they took 'em all down so Jerry wun't know where he was,' said the boy. He had a line of small stones on the kerb beside him. Every so often he'd pick one up and throw it with great accuracy at a tin can on the other side of the road.

'Who's Jerry?'

One eye looked at him with deep suspicion.

'The *Germans*,' said the boy. 'Only I wants 'em to come here and blow up Mrs Density a bit.'

'Why? Are we fighting the Germans?' said Wobbler.

'Are you 'n American? Our dad says the Americans ought to fight, only they're waitin' to see who's winnin'.'

'Er . . . ' Wobbler decided it might be best to be American for a bit. 'Yes. Sure.'

'Garn! Say something American!'

'Er . . . right on. Republican. Microsoft. Spiderman. Have a nice day.'

This demonstration of transatlantic origins

seemed to satisfy the small boy. He threw another stone at the tin can.

'Our mam said I've got to stop along of Mrs Density's and the food's all *rubbish*,' said the boy. 'You know what, she makes me drink *milk*! I dint mind the proper milk at home but round here, you know what, it comes out of a cow's *bum*. I seen it. They took us to a farm with all muck all over the place and, you know what, you know how eggs come out? Urrr! And she makes us go to bed at seven o'clock and I miss our mam and I'm going home. I've had enough of being 'vacuated!'

'It can really make your arm ache,' said Wobbler. 'I had it done for tetanus.'

'Our Ron says it's good fun, going down the Underground station when the siren goes off,' the boy went on. 'Our Ron says the school got hit an' none of the kids has to go any more.'

It seemed to Wobbler that it didn't matter what he said. The boy was really talking to himself. Another stone turned the can upside down.

'Huh,' said the boy. 'Like to see 'em hit the school *here*. They just pick on us just 'cos we're from London and, you know what, that Atterbury kid pinched my piece of shrapnel! Our Ron give it me. Our Ron's a copper, he gets a chance to pick up really good stuff for me. You don't get shrapnel round here, huh!'

'What's shrapnel?' said Wobbler.

'Are you a loony? It's bits of bomb! Our Ron says Alf Harvey got a whole collection *an'* a bit off'f a

Heinkel. Our Ron said Alf Harvey found a real Nazi ring with an actual finger still in it.' The boy looked wistful, as though unfairly shut off from untold treasures. 'Huh! Our Ron says other kids down our street have gone back home and I reckon I'm old enough, too, so I'm goin'.'

Wobbler had never bothered much with history. As far as he was concerned it was something that had happened to other people.

He vaguely remembered a TV programme with some film shot back in the days when people were so poor they could only afford to be in black and white.

Kids with labels round their necks, waiting at railway stations. Every single adult wearing a hat . . .

Evacuees, that was it. Sent out from the big cities so's they wouldn't get bombed, it said.

'What year's this?' he said.

The boy looked at him sideways.

'You're a spy, incha,' he said, standing up. 'You don't know anyfink about nuffink. You ain't American 'cos I seen 'em on the pictures. If you're'n American, where's your gun?'

'Don't be daft, Americans don't all have guns,' said Wobbler. 'Lots of them don't have guns. Well . . . some don't, anyway.'

'Our Ron said there was something in the paper about German parachuters landing disguised as nuns,' said the boy, backing away. 'Seems to *me* you could've been a parachuter, if it was a big parachute.'

'All right, I'm English,' said Wobbler.

'Oh, yeah? Who's the Prime Minster, then?'

Wobbler hesitated.

'I don't think we've done that at school,' he said.

'You don't get no lessons in knowing about Winston Churchill,' said the boy dismissively.

'Hah, you're just trying to mess me around,' said Wobbler. ''Cos I know for a *fact* we've never had a black Prime Minister.'

'You don't know *nuffink*,' said the boy, grabbing his battered suitcase. '*And* you're fat.'

'I don't have to stand here listening to you,' said Wobbler, heading off down the road.

'Spy spy spy,' said the boy.

'Oh, shut up.'

'*An*' you wobble. I saw that Goering on the newsreels. You look *jus*' like him. *An*' you're dressed up all funny. Spy spy spy!'

Wobbler sighed. He was fairly used to this, only not so much these days because once he'd just been fat and now he was *big* and fat.

'And *you're* stupid,' he said. 'But at least *I* could get slimmer.'

Biting sarcasm didn't work.

'Spy spy spy! Nasty nasty Nazi!'

Wobbler tried walking faster.

'I'm goin' to tell Mrs Density an' she can telephone our Ron and he can come an' arrest you!' shouted the boy, jumping along behind him.

Wobbler tried walking faster still.

'He's got a *gun*, our Ron.'

A man went by slowly on his bike.

'He's a spy,' said the boy, pointing at Wobbler. 'I'm arresting him for our Ron.'

The man just grinned at Wobbler and pedalled onwards.

'Our Ron says you spies send Morse code messages to Nazi submarines by flashing torches,' said the boy.

'We're twenty miles from the sea,' said Wobbler, who'd almost broken into a run.

'You could stand on something high. Nyer nyer nyer. Spy spy spy.'

It was just plain stupid, thought Bigmac, as he watched the two plumes of steam in front of him.

What kind of idiots built a car without power steering or synchromesh gears and put in brakes apparently operated by string? He was practically doing the world a favour by taking the car off the road.

Not just off the road, in fact, but over the pavement and across a flowerbed and into the Alderman Bowler Memorial Horsetrough.

The plumes of steam were quite pretty, really. There were little rainbows in them.

'Well, now,' said a voice, as someone opened a car door, 'what do we have here?'

'I think I banged my head,' said Bigmac.

A large hand encircled his arm and pulled him out of the car. Bigmac looked up into two round faces that had 'policeman' written all over them.

There was room for quite a lot of things to be written all over them. They were very large faces.

'That is Dr Roberts' car,' they said, 'and you, my lad, are in for it. What's your name?'

'Simon Wrigley,' mumbled Bigmac. 'Ms Partridge knows all about me . . .'

'She does, does she? And who's she?'

Bigmac blinked at the two faces which miraculously flowed together and became one.

He'd quite liked Ms Partridge. She was nasty. The two social workers he'd had before had made out that he was wet, whereas Ms Partridge made it clear that if she had her way Bigmac would have been strangled at birth. You could *respect* someone like that. They didn't make you feel like some kind of a useless nerd.

Something prodded at his memory.

'When is this?' he said, rubbing his head.

'You can start by telling me where you live—' The policeman leaned closer. There was something about Bigmac that bothered him.

'What do you mean, when is this?' he said.

'What year?'

The policeman had fairly fixed ideas about what should happen to car thieves, but they usually knew what year it was.

'It's 1941,' he said, and straightened up. His eyes narrowed.

'Who's the captain of the England cricket team?' he said.

Bigmac blinked.

'What? How should I know?'

'Who won the Boat Race last year?'

'What boat race?'

The policeman looked again.

'And what's that on your belt?'

Bigmac blinked again, and looked down.

'I didn't nick it,' he said quickly. 'It's only a transistor, anyway.'

'What's that wire going into your ear?'

'Don't be daft. It's only the earphone—'

The policeman's hand landed on his shoulder with the kind of thud that suggested it wasn't going to let go in a hurry.

'You come along with me, Fritz,' he said. 'I wasn't born yesterday.'

Bigmac's brain drifted into focus. He looked at the uniform, and at the crowd behind it, and it began to dawn on him that he was all alone and a long, long way from home.

'I wasn't born yesterday, either,' he said. 'Does that help?'

Johnny, Kirsty and Yo-less sat in a little garden. As far as Johnny could tell, it was where part of the ring road and a traffic island were going to be one day. Now it contained a bench and some geraniums.

'They'll blow up Paradise Street tonight,' said Johnny.

'Where's that?' said Yo-less.

'Here. It's where the sports centre was . . . will be, I mean.'

'Never heard of it.'

'Yes. I did *say*. It got blown up. And you know the funny thing about it?'

'There's something funny about it?' said Kirsty.

'It was by accident! The Germans had meant to bomb the big goods yard at Slate! But they got a bit lost and the weather turned bad and they saw the railway yards here and dropped all their bombs and went home. Everyone was in bed because the air raid sirens didn't go off in time!'

'All right, all right, I know, you've told me before, and all about Adolf and Stalin. It's very sad but you shouldn't get worked up about it,' said Kirsty. 'It's history. That sort of thing happens in history.'

'Aren't you listening? It hasn't happened *yet*. This is *now*. It's going to happen *tonight*.'

They stared at the geraniums.

'Why haven't we gone back yet?' said Kirsty. 'We've been here *ages*.'

'How should I know?' said Johnny. 'Maybe the further you go, the longer you stay.'

'*And* we just happened to go to somewhere you know all about,' said Yo-less. 'That's a bit strange, in my opinion.'

It had worried Johnny, too. Everything *felt* real, but maybe he'd just gone mad and taken everyone else with him.

'I don't want to stay here, that's definite,' said Yo-less. 'Being Little Black Sambo wasn't my idea of a full life.'

Johnny stood up and grasped the handles of the trolley.

'I'm going to see Paradise Street,' he said.

'That's a very bad idea,' said Kirsty. 'I told you, anything you do affects the future.'

'I'm only going to have a look.'

'Oh yes? I find that very hard to believe, actually.'

'She's right,' said Yo-less, trying to keep up. 'You shouldn't mess around with Time. I read this book where a man went right back in time and trod on . . . on a dinosaur, and changed the whole future.'

'A dinosaur?' said Kirsty.

'I think it was a dinosaur. Maybe they had small ones.'

'Huh. Or he was a very big man, perhaps,' said Kirsty.

The trolley bumped off the pavement, rattled across a road, and clanked up the pavement on the other side.

'What're you going to do?' said Kirsty. 'Knock on people's doors and say, "Excuse me, some bombers are going to bomb this street tonight"?'

'Why not?'

'Because they'll lock you up, that's why,' said Yo-less.

'Right,' said Kirsty. 'It'll be just like the man who trod on Yo-less's dinosaur.'

'It may have been some sort of insect, now I come to think of it,' said Yo-less. 'Anyway, there's nothing you can do. It's already happened, otherwise how come you know about it? You can't mess up history.'

The trolley stopped so quickly that they ran into the back of Johnny.

'Why does everyone always talk like that?' he said. 'It's *stupid*. You would really watch someone run over by a car because that's what was supposed to happen, would you? Everything we do changes the future, all the time. So we ought to do what's *right*.'

'Don't shout, people are looking at us,' said Kirsty.

The trolley bumped over the kerb and started to bounce on some cobbles. They were already out of the town centre.

And there was Paradise Street.

It wasn't very long. There were only ten terraced houses on either side, and some of them were boarded up. The far end was a pair of double wooden gates to a factory. They'd once been painted green, but time and the weather had turned the colour into a sort of mossy grey.

Someone had chalked a set of goalposts on the doors, and half a dozen small boys in knee-length shorts were kicking a ball about.

Johnny watched them as they scuffled and perpetrated fouls that would have gladdened the heart of any football manager.

About halfway along the street a young man was repairing a motorcycle. Tools lay on a piece of sacking on the pavement. The football emerged from a complicated tackle, hit the spanners, and almost knocked the bike over.

'Turn it up, you little devils,' said the man, pushing the ball away.

'You never said anything about children,' said Kirsty, so quietly that Johnny nearly didn't hear her.

Johnny shrugged.

'It's *all* going to get blown up?' said Yo-less.

Johnny nodded.

'There wasn't very much detail in the local paper,' he said. 'They didn't used to put very much in, in case the enemy read it. It was all to do with something they called the war effort. You know .... not wanting to let the enemy know you'd been hurt. There was a photo of a lady with her thumb up saying "Blackbury can take it, Mister Hitler!" but there was hardly anything else about the raid until a couple of years afterwards.'

'You mean the government hushed it up?' said Kirsty.

'Makes sense, I suppose,' said Yo-less gloomily. 'I mean, you don't want to say to the enemy, "Hey, you missed your target, have another go".'

The football slammed against the factory gates, rattling them. There didn't seem to be any teams. The ball just went everywhere, surrounded by a mob of small boys.

'I don't see what we could *do*,' said Kirsty. Her voice sounded uneasy, now.

'What? Just now you were telling me I *shouldn't* do anything,' said Johnny.

'It's different when you see people, isn't it?'

'Yes.'

'I suppose it *wouldn't* work if we just told some-one?'

'They'd say "how do you know?" and then you'd probably get shot as a spy,' said Yo-less. 'They used to shoot spies.'

7

Heavy Mental

The man in the khaki uniform turned Bigmac's transistor radio over and over in his hands.

Bigmac watched nervously. There was a police sergeant in the room, and Bigmac was familiar with policemen. But there was a soldier standing by the door, and he had a gun in a holster. And the one sitting down looked tired but had a very sharp expression. Bigmac was not the fastest of thinkers, but it had dawned on him that this was unlikely to be the kind of situation where you got let off with a caution.

'Let's start again,' said the seated soldier, who had introduced himself as Captain Harris. 'Your name is . . . ?'

Bigmac hesitated. He wanted to say, 'You get Ms Partridge, she'll sort it all out, it's not my fault, she says I'm socially dysfunctional', but there was an expression on the captain's face that suggested that this might be a very unfortunate move.

'Simon Wrigley.'

'And you say you are fourteen years old and live in—' Captain Harris glanced at his notes, 'the Joshua Che N'Clement "block" which is near here, you say.'

'You can see it easily,' said Bigmac, trying to be helpful. 'Or you could do, if it was here.'

The captain and the police sergeant glanced at one another.

'It's not here?' said the captain.

'Yes. I don't know why,' said Bigmac.

'Tell me again what Heavy Mental is,' said the captain.

'They're a neo-punk thrash band,' said Bigmac.

'A music band?'

'Er, yes.'

'And we would have heard them on the wireless, perhaps?'

'I shouldn't think so,' said Bigmac. 'Their last single was "I'm going to rip off your head and spit down the hole".'

'"Rip off your head—"' said the policeman, who was taking notes.

'"—and spit down the hole",' said Bigmac helpfully.

'This watch of yours with the numbers on it,' said the captain. 'I see it's got little buttons, too. What happens if I press them?'

The policeman tried to move away a little.

'The one on the left lights it up so you can see it in the dark,' said Bigmac.

'Really? And why would you want to do that?'

'When you wake up in the night and want to know what time it is?' Bigmac suggested, after some deep thought.

'I see. And the other button?'

'Oh, that's to tell you what time it is in another country.'

Everyone suddenly seemed very interested.

'What other country?' said the captain sharply.

'It's stuck on Singapore,' said Bigmac.

The captain laid it down very carefully. The sergeant wrote out a label and tied it to the watch strap. Then the captain picked up Bigmac's jacket.

'What is this made of?' he said.

'I dunno. Some kind of plastic,' said Bigmac. 'They sell them down the market.'

The captain pulled it this way and that.

'How is it made?'

'Ah, I know that,' said Bigmac. 'I read about it. You mix some chemicals together, and you get plastic. Easy.'

'In camouflage colours,' said the captain.

Bigmac licked his lips. He was sure that he was in deep trouble, so there was no sense in pretending.

'That's just to make you look hard,' he said.

'Hard. I see,' said the captain, and his eyes didn't give away whether he really saw or not. He held up the back of the jacket and pointed to two words done rather badly in biro.

'What exactly are BLACKBURY SKINS?' he said.

'Er. That's me and Bazza and Skazz. Er. Skinheads. A . . . kind of gang . . . '

'Gang,' said the captain.

'Er. Yes.'

'Skinheads?'

'Er . . . the haircut,' said Bigmac.

'Looks like an ordinary military haircut to me,' said the sergeant.

'And these,' said the captain, pointing to the swastikas on either side of the name. 'Gang badges, are they? Also to make you look . . . hard?'

'Er . . . it's just . . . you know . . . Adolf Hitler and that,' said Bigmac.

All the men were staring at him.

'It's just decoration,' said Bigmac.

The captain put the coat down very slowly.

'It's nothing to get *excited* about,' said Bigmac. 'Where I come from, you can buy badges and things down the market, you can get Gestapo knives—'

'That's enough!' said the captain. 'Now listen to me. You'll make it easier on yourself if you tell me the truth right now. I want your name, the names of your contacts . . . everything. A unit is coming from headquarters and they aren't as patient as I am, do you understand?'

He stood up and started to put Bigmac's labelled belongings into a sack.

'Hey, that's my stuff—' mumbled Bigmac.

'Lock him up.'

'You can't lock me up just for some old car—'

'We can for spying,' said Captain Harris. 'Oh, yes, we can.'

He strode out of the room.

'Spying?' said Bigmac. 'Me?'

'Are you one of them Hitler Youths?' said the sergeant, conversationally. 'I saw you lot on the newsreel. Waving all them torches. Nasty pieces of work, I thought. Like Boy Scouts gone bad.'

'I haven't spied for anyone!' shouted Bigmac. 'I don't know how to spy! I don't even like Germany! My brother got sent home from Munich for stitching up one of their football supporters with a scaffolding pole even though it wasn't his fault!'

Such rock-solid evidence of anti-Germanic feeling did not seem to impress the sergeant.

'You can get shot, you know,' he said. 'For the first offence.'

The door was still open. Bigmac could hear noises in the corridor. Someone was talking on the phone, somewhere in the distance.

Bigmac wasn't an athlete. If there was an Olympic Sick Note event, he would have been in the British team. He would've won the 100 metres I've Got Asthma, the half-marathon Lurk in the Changing Rooms, and the freestyle Got to Go to the Doctor.

But his boots dug into the floor and he rose out of his chair like a missile going off. His feet barely touched the table top. He went past the policeman's shoulder with his legs already making running motions. Fear gave him superhuman acceleration. Ms Partridge might make cutting remarks but she wasn't allowed to use bullets however much she wanted to.

Bigmac landed in the doorway, turned at random, put his head down and charged. It was a hard head. It hit someone around belt level. There was a shout and a crash.

He saw another gap and headed for it. There was another crash, and the sound of a telephone smashing on the floor. Someone yelled at him to halt or they'd fire.

Bigmac didn't stop to find out what'd happened. He just hoped that a pair of 1990s Doc Martens that had been practically bought legally by his brother off a man with a lorry full of them were *much* better for dodging and running than huge police boots.

Whoever had been shouting stop or they'd fire . . . fired.

There was a *crack* and a clang somewhere ahead of Bigmac, but he turned down a corridor, ran under the outstretched arms of another policeman, and out into a yard.

A policeman was standing next to a Jurassic bicycle, a huge machine that looked as if it were made of drainpipes welded together.

Bigmac went past him in a blur, grabbed the handlebars, swung onto the saddle and rammed his feet onto the pedals.

"'Ere, what're you doin'—'

The policeman's voice faded behind him.

The bike swung out into the lane behind the station.

It was a cobbled street. The saddle was solid

leather. Bigmac's trousers were very thin.

'No wonder everyone was very depressed,' he thought, trying to cycle standing up.

'Nyer nyer nyer. Spy spy spy.'

'Shut up!' said Wobbler. 'Why don't you run away to London?'

'Ain't gonna run away to London *now*,' said the boy. ''S'lot more fun catchin' spies *here*.'

They were back in the heart of the town now. The boy trailed behind Wobbler, pointing him out to passers-by. Admittedly, no-one seemed to be about to arrest him, but he was getting some odd looks.

'My brother Ron's a *policeman*,' said the boy. 'He'll come up from London and shoot you with his *gun*.'

'Go away!'

'Sharn't!'

Opposite the entrance to Paradise Street was a small church. It was a non-conformist chapel, according to Yo-less. It had a shut-up, wet Sunday look. A couple of elderly evergreen trees on either side of the door looked as though it'd take a shovel just to get the soot off their leaves.

The three of them sat on the steps, watching the street. A woman had come out and was industriously scrubbing her doorstep.

'Did this chapel get hit?' said Kirsty.

'You mean *will*. I don't think so.'

'Pity.'

'It's still here . . . I mean, in 1996,' said Yo-less. 'Only it's just used as a social hall. You know, for keep-fit classes and stuff. I know, 'cos I come here for Morris Dance practice every Wednesday. Will, I mean.'

'You?' said Kirsty. '*You* do Morris Dancing? With sticks and hankies and stuff? *You?*'

'There's something wrong?' said Yo-less coldly.

'Well . . . no . . . no, of course not . . . but . . . it's just an unusual interest for someone of - your—'

Yo-less let her squirm for a bit and then said, 'Height?' He dropped the word like a weight. Kirsty shut her mouth.

'Yes,' she said.

Another woman appeared, next door to the one scrubbing her front doorstep, and started scrubbing *her* doorstep.

'What are we going to *do*?' said Kirsty.

'I'm thinking,' said Yo-less.

Somewhere in the distance a bell went off, and kept on going off.

'I'm thinking, too,' said Johnny. 'I'm thinking: we haven't seen Bigmac for ages.'

'Good,' said Kirsty.

'He might be in some trouble, I mean,' said Johnny.

'What do you mean, *might* be?' said Yo-less.

'And we haven't seen Wobbler, either,' said Johnny.

124

'Oh, you know Wobbler. He's probably hiding somewhere.'

Another woman opened the door on the other side of the street and entered the doorstep-scrubbing competition.

Kirsty straightened up.

'Why're we acting so miserable?' she said. 'We're Nineties people. We should be able to think of something. We could . . . we could . . .'

'We could ring up Adolf Hitler,' Yo-less suggested. 'Can't remember his phone number, sorry, but directory inquiries in Germany're *bound* to know.'

Johnny stared glumly at the shopping trolley. He hadn't expected time travel to be this hard. He thought of all those wasted lessons when they could have been telling him what to do if some mad woman left him a trolley full of time. School never taught you anything that was useful in real life. There probably wasn't a single text book that told you what to do if it turned out you were living next door to Elvis Presley.

He looked down the length of Paradise Street, and felt Time streaming past him. Yo-less and Kirsty faded away. He could *feel* them there, though, as insubstantial as dreams, as the light faded from the sky and the footballers went indoors and the wind got up and the clouds rolled in from the south-west and the town went to sleep and the bombers came out of the east and fire rained down on the houses and the allotments and the people and the goalposts chalked on the wall and all the nice, clean, white doorsteps . . .

Captain Harris turned Bigmac's watch over.

'Amazing,' he said. 'And it says "Made In Japan".'

'Fiendishly cunning,' said the police sergeant.

The captain picked up the radio.

'Japanese again,' he said. 'Why? Why put it on the back? See here. Made in Japan.'

'I thought it was all rice,' said the sergeant. 'That's what my dad said. He was out there.'

Captain Harris fiddled one of the tiny head-phones into his ear and moved a switch. He listened to the hiss that was due to be replaced by Radio Blackbury in forty-eight years' time, and nodded.

'It's doing *something*,' he said. His thumb touched the wavechange switch, and he blinked.

'It's the Home Service,' he said. 'Clear as a bell!'

'We could have the back off it in no time,' said the sergeant.

'No,' said Sergeant Harris. 'This has got to go to the Ministry. The men in white coats can have a look at it. How can you get valves to fit in this? Where's the aerial?'

'Very small feet,' said the sergeant.

'Sorry, sergeant?'

'That's what my dad said. Japanese. The women. Very small feet, he said. So maybe they've got small hands, too. Just a thought.' The sergeant tried to extend his line of technological speculation. 'Good for making small things? You know. Like ships in bottles?'

The captain put the tiny radio back in the box.

'I've seen people do them,' said the sergeant, still anxious to be of assistance. 'You get a bottle, then you get a lot of very thin thread—'

'He's the best actor I've ever seen, I know that,' said Captain Harris. 'You could really think he was just a stupid boy. But this stuff . . . I just can't believe it. It's all very . . . odd.'

'We've got every man out after him,' said the sergeant. 'And the inspector has called out the army from West Underton. We'll have him in no time.'

The captain sealed the box with sticky tape.

'I want this guarded,' he said.

'We'll keep an eye on it in the main office.'

'No. I want it secure.'

'Well, there's an empty cell. Actually there's someone in it but I'll soon have 'em out.'

'More secure than that.'

The sergeant scratched an ear.

'There's the Lost Property cupboard,' he said. 'But there's important stuff in it—'

'Lost Property cupboard! Haven't you got a safe?'

'No.'

'What'd happen if the Crown Jewels were found in the gutter, then?'

'We'd put 'em in the Lost Property cupboard,'

said the sergeant promptly. 'And then ring up the King. If his name was in them, of course. Look, it's a good thick door and there's only one key and I've got it.'

'All right, take out what's in there and put it in your cell and put the box in the cupboard,' said the captain.

'Chief Inspector won't like that. Very important stuff, Lost Property.'

'Tell him we can co-operate in a very friendly fashion now or if he prefers he can take a call from the Chief Constable in two minutes,' said Captain Harris, putting his hand on the phone. 'One way or the other, hmm?'

The sergeant looked worried. 'You serious about this, sir?' he said.

'Oh, yes.'

'That stuff's not going to go off bang or anything, is it?'

'I'm not sure. I don't think so.'

Five minutes later the sergeant walked down to the cells with his arms full of the contents of the cupboard, and a put-upon expression on his face. He put them on a bench in the corridor and fished out his keys. Then he pulled aside the hatch in a cell door.

'You all right, old girl?'

'That's what *you* think. Talk about a blue pencil! You can tell he's a lad, can't yer, Mister Shadwell?'

'Yes, yes,' said the sergeant, opening the door.

The old lady sat on the bed. She was so short that her feet swung several inches above the floor. And there was a cat on her lap. It growled when it saw the sergeant – a slow, rising growl which suggested that, if there was any attempt to pick the cat up, it was all going to end in claws.

The sergeant had long ago stopped worrying about how the cat could get into the cells. It happened every time. There wasn't room via the windows and it certainly couldn't have got in through the door, but every night the old lady was in the cells, the cat would be in there, too, in the morning.

'Finished your breakfast, have you?'

'Millennium hand and shrimp,' said Mrs Tachyon happily.

'Good. Then you just come along with me. It's a nice day outside,' said the sergeant.

'Beam me up, Scotty,' said Mrs Tachyon, standing up and following him obediently. The sergeant shook his head sadly.

She trailed behind him into the station yard where, under a bit of canvas the sergeant had thrown over it the night before, there was a wire trolley loaded down with bags.

Mrs Tachyon looked at it.

'No-one nicked anything?' she said.

She was like that, the sergeant thought. Mad as a hatter most of the time and then suddenly a sentence'd come out at you like a razor blade in candy floss.

'Now then, old love, as if anyone'd touch that lot,' he said, as kindly as possible.

'Points win prizes. Hats.'

The sergeant reached under the trolley and produced a pair of boots.

'These belonged to my mum,' he said. 'She was going to throw 'em out, but I said, there's still some good leather on them—'

Mrs Tachyon snatched them out of his hand. In seconds they were somewhere in the pile of bags on the trolley.

'It's a small step for a man,' said Mrs Tachyon.

'Yes, they're size sixes,' said the sergeant.

'Ah, Bisto. It's a great life if yer don't weaken, but of course they've put a bridge there now.'

The sergeant looked down at the trolley.

'Dunno where you get this stuff from,' he said. 'What're these bags made of, love? Looks like rubber or something.'

'Obbly Obbly Ob. Weeeed!' said Mrs Tachyon. 'I told them, but no-one listens to a teapot. Fab!'

The sergeant sighed, put his hand in his pocket and produced a sixpence.

'Get yourself a cup of tea and a bun,' he said.

'Hats. That's what *you* think,' said Mrs Tachyon, taking it.

'Don't mention it.'

The sergeant headed back into the police station.

He was *used* to Mrs Tachyon. When nights were cold you'd sometimes hear a milk bottle smash on the step outside. This was technically a crime, and it meant that Mrs Tachyon was looking for somewhere warm for the night.

Not on *every* cold night, though. That was a puzzler, and no mistake. Last winter it had been very nippy indeed for quite a long time and the lads had got a bit worried. It came as quite a relief when they'd heard the crash of breaking glass and the cry of 'I *told* 'em! That's what *you* think!' Mrs Tachyon came and went, and no-one knew where she came from, and you never found out where she'd gone . . .

Beam me up, Snotty? Mad as a hatter, of course.

But . . . strange, too. Like, after you'd given her something you ended up feeling as if she'd done you a favour.

He heard the rattle of the trolley behind him, and then a sudden silence.

He turned around. The trolley, and Mrs Tachyon, had gone.

Johnny felt the *hereness* of here. It'd happen *here*, not in some far-off country full of odd names and foreign people with thick moustaches shouting slogans.

It'd happen *here*, where there were public libraries and zebra crossings and people who did the football pools.

Bombs would come crashing through roofs and ceilings and down to the cellars, and turn the world white.

And it would happen, because as Yo-less said, it *had* happened. It was going to have happened, and he couldn't possibly stop it, because if he *did* find some way of stopping it, then he wouldn't know about it happening, would he?

Maybe Mrs Tachyon collected Time. Johnny felt in a way that he couldn't quite put into words that Time wasn't just something that was on clocks and calendars but lived in people's heads, too. And if that meant you had to think like this, no wonder she sounded mad.

'Are you all right?' said a voice, a long way away.

Miraculously, the rubble became houses again, the light came up, the football rattled against the goal in the warm afternoon air.

Kirsty waved a hand in front of his face.

'Are you OK?'

'I was just . . . thinking,' said Johnny.

'I hate it when you switch off like that.'

'Sorry.'

Johnny stood up.

'We didn't come back here by accident,' he said. 'I was thinking a lot about tonight, and we ended up coming here just in time. I don't know why. But we've got to do something, even if there's nothing we can do. So I'm going to—'

A bicycle came around the corner. It was bouncing up and down on the cobbles and the skinny figure riding it was a mere blur. It clanked to a halt in front of them.

They stared at the cyclist. He was shaking so much he looked slightly out of focus.

'Bigmac?'

'Ur-ur-ur—' shuddered Bigmac.

'How many fingers am I holding up?' said Kirsty.

'Ur-ur-ur-n-n-nineteen? H-h-hide the bike!'

'Why?' said Kirsty.

'I didn't do anything!'

'Ah,' said Yo-less, knowingly. 'It's like that, is it?'

He picked up the bike and wheeled it into the sooty shrubs.

'Like what?' said Kirsty, looking bewildered.

'Bigmac *always* never does anything,' said Johnny.

'That's right,' said Yo-less. 'There can't be anyone in the whole universe who's got into so much trouble for things he didn't do in places he wasn't at that weren't his fault.'

'Th-th-they *shot* at me!'

'Wow!' said Yo-less. 'You must've not done anything really *big* this time!'

'Th-there was th-this c-car—'

The ringing Johnny had heard before started again, somewhere behind the buildings.

'Th-that's a police car!' said Bigmac. 'I tried to give them the slip down Harold Wilson Drive and – it wasn't there! And one of them shot at me! With an actual gun! Soldiers aren't supposed to shoot people!'

They dragged the trembling Bigmac into the horrible bushes. Kirsty gave him her mac to stop him shivering.

'All right, game over. I said game over!' he moaned. 'Let's pack it in, all right? Let's go home!'

'I think we should try to tell people about the bombs,' Johnny said. 'Someone might listen.'

'And if they ask how do you know, you'll say you're from 1996, will you?'

'Maybe you could . . . you know . . . write a note,' said Yo-less. 'Slip it into someone's letter-box?'

'Oh, yes?' said Kirsty, hotly. 'What should we write? "Go for a long walk" perhaps? Or "Wear a very hard hat"?'

She stopped when she saw Johnny's expression.

'Sorry,' she said. 'I didn't mean that.'

'Wobbler!' said Yo-less.

They turned. Wobbler was toiling along the street. It took some effort for Wobbler to manage a run, but when he did so, there was also something terribly unstoppable about him.

He spotted them, and changed direction.

'Am I glad to see you,' he panted. 'Let's get out of here! Some loony kid chased me all the way down the hill. He kept shouting out that I was a spy!'

'Did he try to shoot you?' said Bigmac.

'He threw stones!'

'Hah! *I* got shot at!' said Bigmac, with a sort of pride.

'All right,' said Kirsty. 'We're all here. Let's go.'

'You *know* I don't know how!' said Johnny.

The bags lay there in the trolley. There were the words 'Shop At Tescos' on a piece of metal on the front of the wire. Probably Mr Tesco just owned a tiny grocery shop or something back here, Johnny thought wildly. Or hadn't been born yet.

'It's your mind that works it,' said Kirsty. 'It must be. You go where you're thinking.'

'Oh, come *on*,' said Yo-less. 'That's like *magic*.'

Johnny stared at the trolley again. 'I could . . . try,' he said.

A police car went by, a street away.

'Let's get somewhere more hidden,' said Yo-less.

'Good idea,' muttered Bigmac.

A cinder path went around the back of the little church, to an area with dustbins and a heap of dead flowers. There was a small green door. It opened easily.

'In those – in these days, they didn't lock churches,' said Yo-less.

'But there's silver candlesticks and stuff, isn't there?' said Bigmac. 'Anyone could walk right in and nick 'em.'

'Don't,' said Johnny.

They manhandled the trolley into a back room. It contained a tea urn on a trestle table, a pile of battered hymnbooks, and not much else except the smell of old embroidery, furniture polish and stale air, which is known as the odour of sanctity. There was no sign of any silver candlesticks any-where—

'Bigmac! Shut that cupboard!' said Yo-less.

'I was only *looking*.'

Johnny stared at the sacks. All right, he thought. Let's say they're full of time. It's a daft idea. After all, they're quite small sacks—

On the other hand, how much space does time take up?

Perhaps it's compressed . . . folded up . . .

Mrs Tachyon collects time like other old ladies collect string?

This is daft.

But . . .

There was a deep, rumbling sound. Guilty had sat up in the trolley and was purring happily.

Johnny took a sack and held it carefully by the neck. It felt warm, and he was sure it moved slightly under his grip.

'This probably won't work,' he said.

'Should we hold on to the trolley?' said Yo-less.

'I don't think so. I don't know! Look, are you all sure? I really don't know what I'm doing!'

'Yes, but you've never really known what you're doing, have you?' said Kirsty.

'That's right,' said Yo-less. 'So you've had a lot of practice.'

Johnny shut his eyes and tried to think of . . . 1996.

The thought crept into his mind from somewhere outside. It's not a time, it's a *place*.

It's a place where the model of the Space Shuttle on the ceiling hangs by a bit of red wool because you ran out of black thread.

And the model's got streaks of glue on it because you always get it wrong somewhere.

It's a place where your mum just smokes a lot and looks out of the window.

It's a place where your grandad watches TV all day.

It's *where you want to be*.

His mind began to go fuzzy at the edges. He thought of Thomas the Tank Engine wallpaper and the Mr Men lamp, until they were so close he could almost taste them. He could *hear* the place where Grandad had hung the wallpaper wrong so that there was an engine that was half Thomas and half James. It hung like a beacon in his head.

He opened his eyes. The images were still around him; the others looked like ghosts. They were staring at him.

He opened the bag, just a fraction.

Wobbler swallowed.

'Er . . . ' he said.

He turned around. And then, just in case, he looked behind the table.

'Er . . . guys? Johnny? Bigmac? Yo-less?' He swallowed again, but sometimes you just had to face up to unpleasant facts, and so he bravely said: 'Er . . . *Kirsty?*'

No-one answered. There was no-one *there* to answer.

He was all alone with the tea urn.

'Hey, I was even holding on!' he said. 'Oi! I'm still here! Very funny, ha ha, now joke over, all right? Guys? Johnny? You've left me *behind*! All right? It worked, yes. Joke over, ha ha ha, all right? Please?'

He opened the door and looked out into the shadowy yard.

'I know you're only doing this to wind me up, well, it hasn't worked,' he moaned.

Then he went back and sat on a bench with his hands on his lap.

After a while he fished out a grubby paper handkerchief and blew his nose. He was about to throw it away when he stopped and glared at it. It was probably the only paper handkerchief in the *world*.

'I can see you peering out at me,' he said, but his heart wasn't in it. 'You're going to jump out any minute, I know. Well, it's not working. 'Cos I'm not worried, see. Let's all go home and get a burger, eh? Good idea, eh? Tell you what, I've got some money, I don't mind buyin' 'em, eh? Hey? Or we could go down the Chinese and get a take-away—'

He stopped, and looked exactly like someone who'd realized that it was going to be a long, long time before there were any beansprouts in this town. Or burgers, come to that. All there probably was to eat was meat and fish and stuff.

'All right, fair enough, you can come out now
. . .'

A fly stirred on the windowsill, and started to bang itself absentmindedly on the glass.

'Look, it's not funny any m . . . more, all right?'

There was a movement of air behind him, and a definite sensation that, where there had been no-one, there was now someone.

Wobbler turned around, a huge relieved grin on his face.

'Ha, I bet you thought you'd got me going – *what?*'

The Over-50s' Keep-Fit class was in full wheeze. The tutor had long ago given up expecting everyone to keep up, so she just pressed on in the hope that people would do what they could manage and, if possible, not actually die while on the premises.

'And *bend* and *bend* and *bend* and – do the best you can, Miss Windex – *step* and *step* and – what?'

She blinked.

Johnny looked around.

The keep-fit class, after ten minutes of aerobics, were not the most observant people. One or two of them actually made space for the newcomers.

The tutor hesitated. She'd been brought up to believe in a healthy mind in a healthy body, and, since she was pretty sure she had a healthy body, it was not possible, she reasoned, that a group of people and an overloaded shopping trolley could have suddenly appeared at the back of the old church hall. They must have just come in, she reasoned. Admittedly, there was no actual door there, but people certainly didn't just appear out of thin air.

'Where are we?' Kirsty hissed.

'Same place,' whispered Yo-less. 'Different time!'

Even some of the slower fitness fans had caught up by now. The whole class had stopped and turned around and were watching them with interest.

'Well, *say* something!' said Kirsty. 'Everyone's *looking*.'

'Er . . . is this Pottery?' said Johnny.

'What?' said the tutor.

'We're looking for Beginners' Pottery,' said Johnny. It was a wild stab, but every hall and hut and spare room in Blackbury seemed to have its time filled up with people doing weird hobbies or industriously learning Russian.

A small light went on behind the tutor's eyes. She grabbed at the familiar words like a singer snatching a microphone.

'That's Thursdays,' she said. 'In the Red Cross Hall.'

'Oh. Is it? Tch. We're *always* getting it wrong,' said Johnny.

'And after we've lugged all this clay up here, too,' said Yo-less. 'That's a nuisance, isn't it, Bigmac?'

'Don't look at *me*,' said Bigmac. 'They *shot* at me!'

The tutor was staring from one to the other.

'Er. Yes. Well, it can get pretty nasty in Beginners' Pottery,' said Johnny. 'Come on, everyone.'

They all grabbed hold of the trolley. Tracksuited figures limped politely out of the way as it squeaked its way across the floor, bumped down the step and landed in the damp yard outside.

Johnny pushed the door shut behind them, and listened for a moment.

' . . . well, then . . . *bend* and *stretch* and *wheeze* and *bend* . . . '

He straightened up. It was *amazing* what you could get away with. Ten-legged aliens would be immediately accepted in Blackbury if they were bright enough to ask the way to the Post Office and complain about the weather. People had a way of just not seeing anything that common sense said they shouldn't see.

'I bet something's gone wrong,' said Bigmac.

'Er . . . ' said Yo-less.

'No, this has *got* to be the 1990s,' said Kirsty. 'It's the only period in history when you wouldn't be burned at the stake for wearing a green and purple tracksuit, isn't it?'

The bulk of the sports centre loomed opposite them. Five minutes ago, thought Johnny, five of *my* minutes ago, that was a street. Get your head round that.

'Er . . . ' said Yo-less again.

'They *shot* at me,' said Bigmac. 'A *real* bullet! I heard it hit the actual wall!'

'Er . . . ' said Yo-less.

'Oh, what's the *matter* with you?' said Kirsty.

'Er . . . where's Wobbler?'

They looked around.

'Oh, *no* . . . ' said Johnny.

They were Wobblerless.

'I ain't going back!' said Bigmac, backing away. 'Not to get shot at!'

'He wouldn't have wandered off again, would he?' said Kirsty.

'No,' said Johnny. 'He must still be there!'

'Look, get a grip, will you?' said Kirsty. 'You said the church doesn't get hit! He's *OK*.'

'Yes . . . but he's OK in 1941!'

'S'posing something goes wrong?' said Bigmac. '*He* didn't come back this time, s'posing we go back and *all* get stuck? I'll get shot!'

'You think *you've* got problems?' said Yo-less. '*I'd* have to learn to play the banjo.'

'Will you all stop panicking and *think* for a moment?' said Kirsty. 'This is *time* travel. He's always going to be there, *whenever* we go back! Of *course* we ought to go and get him! But we don't have to *rush*.'

Of course, it was true. He'd always be there, thought Johnny. They could go back in ten years' time and he'd still be there. Just like something on a tape – you could play it, and fast forward, and rewind, and it would always be there. And later that night, the bombs would land in Paradise Street – and *that* night would always be there. For ever. Every second, always there. Like little fossils.

Kirsty hauled the trolley away and pushed it down the steps towards the pavement.

'His mum 'n dad'll worry,' said Yo-less, uncertainly.

'No, they won't,' said Kirsty. 'Because we can bring him back to right *here*.'

'Really? Why can't we see us doing it, then?' said Yo-less. 'You mean any minute we're just going to pop up with Wobbler and say "hi, us, here's Wobbler, see you later"?'

'Oh, good grief,' said Kirsty. 'I can't think about that. You can't think about time travel with a logical mind.'

Yo-less turned and looked at Johnny's face.

'Oh, no,' he said, 'He's off again . . .'

Everything's there waiting, Johnny thought. That's the thing about time. It doesn't matter how long it takes to build a time machine. We could all die out and evolution could start again with moles or something, it could take millions of years, but sooner or later someone will find out how to do it. It might not even be a machine. It might just be a way of understanding what time *is*, like everyone was scared of lightning and then one day someone said, look, you can store it in little bottles and then it was just electricity. But it wouldn't actually matter, because once you'd worked out how to use it, everything would be there. If someone ever finds a way of travelling in time, *ever*, in the entire history of the universe, then they could be here today.

And then he thought of the bombers, nosing through the clouds over the houses and the footballers and all those clean doorsteps . . .

'Uh?' he said.

'You all right?' said Yo-less.

'Let's get a drink, at least,' said Kirsty, shoving the trolley firmly towards the town centre.

And then she stopped.

Johnny hadn't often seen her shocked. Kirsty normally dealt with the terrible and the unexpected by getting angry with it. But now she stopped, and went pale.

'Oh, no . . . ' she said.

The road from the old church led down the hill towards traffic lights at the bottom.

An overloaded shopping trolley, with a boy and a girl clinging to it, was hurtling down the other road.

As they watched, it heeled over like a yacht tacking against the wind, turned a full ninety degrees, and plunged into the car park of the Neil Armstrong Shopping Mall.

A long black car followed it.

He'd forgotten all about the car. Maybe there

were secret societies. Maybe there were men in black in long black cars who said things like, 'The truth is out there' and came and found you if you got your hand trapped in the occult.

Johnny could see a map in his head. But it was a map of time.

They'd moved in time at his house. But Yo-less was right, you probably could move in time like a train on a track, so you flipped over onto another track just a little bit further along. You moved in space, really.

And he'd done it again, when he thought they were going to die at the traffic lights. And the black car had vanished . . . because it didn't exist in *this* time. He definitely hadn't seen it when he'd looked behind him.

They'd come back to a time when it existed.

The car pulled to a halt outside the mall.

A feeling of absolute certainty stole over Johnny. He knew the answer. Later on, with any luck, he'd find out what the question was, but right now he was sure of the answer.

Forget about secret societies. Forget about time police. Policemen had to have nice logical minds, and to deal with time you needed a mind like Mrs Tachyon.

But there was someone else who'd *know* where they'd be today, wasn't there . . .

Because . . . supposing we *didn't* go back? Supposing . . . maybe we went back and did things wrong?

He started to run.

Johnny dodged across the road. A car hooted at him.

Across in the car park, a man in black, with black sunglasses and a peaked black hat, got out of the car and hurried into the mall.

Johnny leapt over the low wall into the car park and weaved between shoppers and their trolleys . . .

. . . And panted to a halt in front of the car.

It had stopped right in front of the entrance, where no-one was ever allowed to park.

In the bright sunlight it looked even blacker than Johnny remembered. Its engine ticked occasionally as it cooled down. On the hood was a silver ornament.

It looked very much like a hamburger.

If he squinted, Johnny could just make out a figure in the rear seat, a mere shadow behind the darkness of the glass.

He ran around and snatched at the handle of the back door, yanking it open.

'All right! I know you're in there! Who are you, really?'

Most of the figure was in deep shade, but there was a pair of hands visible, resting on a black cane with a silver tip.

Then the figure moved. It unfolded slowly, and became a large man in a coat that was half coat, half cloak. He emerged carefully, making sure both feet were firmly on the ground before easing the rest of his body out of the car.

He was quite tall, tall enough so that he was big rather than fat. He wore a large black hat and had a short, silvery beard.

He smiled at Johnny, and nodded at the others as they hurried up.

'Who am I?' he said. 'Well, now . . . why don't you guess? You were always good at this sort of thing.'

Johnny looked at him, and then at the car, and then back up the hill to where the old church was just visible.

'I think . . . ' he said.

'Yes?' said the old man. 'Yes? Go on?'

'I think that . . . I mean, I don't know . . . but I know I'm going to know . . . I mean, I think I know why you've come to find us . . . '

'Yes?'

Johnny swallowed. 'But we were—' he began.

The old man patted him on the shoulder.

'Call me Sir John,' he said.

8

Trousers of Time

There were differences in the mall. One big difference, certainly. The burger bar had changed. There were different-shaped paper hats, and the colour scheme was blue and white instead of red and yellow.

The old man led the way.

'Who *is* he?' hissed Kirsty.

'You'll laugh if I tell you! This is *time* travel! I'm still trying to work out the rules!'

Sir John sat down heavily in a seat, motioned them to sit down as well, and then did the second-worst thing anyone could do in a fast-food restaurant.

He snapped his fingers at a waitress.

All the staff were watching them anxiously.

'Young lady,' said Sir John, wheezing slightly, 'these people will have whatever they want. I will have a glass of water. Thank you.'

'Yes, Sir John,' said the waitress, and hurried away.

'You're not s'posed to do that,' said Bigmac hoarsely. 'You're s'posed to queue up.'

'No, *you're* supposed to queue up,' said Sir John. 'I don't have to.'

'Have you always been called Sir John?' said Johnny.

The man winked at him.

'You know, don't you,' he said. 'You've worked it out. You're right. Names are easily changed, especially in wartime. I thought it might be better. I got the knighthood in 1964 for services to making huge amounts of money.'

The waitress hurried back with the water, and then produced a notebook and looked expectantly at them all with the bright, brittle smile of someone who is expecting to be sacked at any moment.

'I'll have . . . well, I'll have everything,' said Yo-less.

'Me too,' said Bigmac.

'Cheeseburger?' said Johnny.

'Chilli beanburger,' said Kirsty. 'And I want to know what's going on, OK?'

Sir John beamed at her in a slightly distracting way. Then he nodded at the waitress.

'Make me one with everything,' he said, slowly and carefully, as if quoting something he'd heard a long time ago, 'because I want to become a Muslim.'

'A *Buddhist*,' said Yo-less, without thinking. 'You *always* muck up the punchl—' Then his mouth dropped open.

'Do I?' said Wobbler.

'Well . . . I hung around for a while and you didn't come back,' said Wobbler. 'And then—'

'But we did! I mean, we will!' said Kirsty.

'This is where it gets difficult,' said Wobbler, patiently. 'Johnny knows. Supposing you didn't go back? Supposing you were scared to, or you found that you couldn't? The possibility exists, and that means the future forks off in two different ways. In one you went back, in one you didn't. Now you've ended up in the future where you didn't go back. I've been here since 1941. Don't try to think too hard about this, because it'll make your brain hurt.

'Anyway . . . *first* I stayed with Mr and Mrs Seeley,' he continued. 'I'd met them that first day. Their son was away in the Navy and everyone thought I was an evacuee who was a bit daft and, what with one thing and another, there's too much to worry about in a big war for people to ask too many questions about one fat boy. They were very nice people. They sort of . . . adopted me, I suppose, because their son got torpedoed. But I moved away after a few years.'

'Why?' said Kirsty.

'I didn't want to meet my own parents or anything like that,' said Wobbler. He still seemed out of breath. 'History is full of patches as it is, without causing any more trouble, eh? Changing my name wasn't hard, either. In a war . . . well, records go missing, people get killed, everything gets shaken up. A person can duck down and pop up somewhere else as *someone* else. I was in the Army for a few years, after the war.'

'*You?*' said Bigmac.

'Oh, everyone had to be. National Service, it was called. Out in Berlin. And then I came back and had to make a living. Would you like another milkshake? I personally wouldn't, if I were you. I know how they're made.'

'You could've invented computers!' said Bigmac.

'Really? You think so?' The old man laughed. 'Who'd have listened to a boy who hadn't even been to university? Besides . . . well, look at this . . .'

He picked up a plastic fork and tapped it on the table.

'See this?' he said. 'We throw away millions of them every day. After five minutes' use they're in the trash, right?'

'Yes, of course,' said Kirsty. Behind Wobbler, the staff were watching nervously, like monks in some quiet monastery somewhere who've just had St Peter drop in for tea.

'A hundred years ago it'd have been a marvel. And now we throw them away without a second thought. So . . . how do you make one?'

'Well . . . you get some oil, and . . . I think there's something about it in a book I've got—'

'Right,' said Wobbler, leaning back. 'You don't know. I don't know, either.'

'But I wouldn't bother with that. *I'd* write science fiction,' said Kirsty. 'Moon landings and stuff.'

'You probably could,' said Wobbler. A tired expression crossed his face, and he started to pat the pockets of his coat as if looking for something. 'But I've never had much of a way with words, I'm afraid. No. I opened a hamburger bar.'

Johnny looked around, and then started to grin.

'That's right,' said Wobbler. 'In 1952. I knew it all, you see. Thick shakes, Double Smashers with Cheese'n Egg, paper hats for the staff, red sauce in those little round plastic bottles that look like tomatoes . . . oh, yes. I had three bars in the first year, and ten the year after that. There's thousands, now. Other people just couldn't keep up. I *knew* what would work, you see. Birthday treats for the kids, the Willie Wobbler clown—'

'*Willie Wobbler?*' said Kirsty.

'Sorry. They were more innocent times,' said Wobbler. 'And then I started . . . other things. Soft toilet paper, for a start. Honestly, the stuff they had back in the 1940s you could use as roofing felt! And when that was going well, I started to listen to people. People with bright ideas. Like "I think I could make a tape recorder *really small* so that people could carry it around" and I'd say "That might just catch on, you know, here's some money to get started". Or "You know, I think I know a way of making a machine to record television signals on tape so that people could watch them later" and I'd say "Amazing! Whatever will they think of next! Here's some money, why don't we form a company and build some? And while we're about it, why don't we see if movies can be put on these tape thingies too?"'

'That's dishonest,' said Kirsty. 'That's *cheating*.'

'I don't see why,' said Wobbler. 'People were amazed that I'd listen to them, because everyone else thought they were crazy. I made money, but so did they.'

'Are you a millionaire?' said Bigmac.

'Oh, no. I was a millionaire back in 1955. I'm a billionaire now, I think.' He snapped his fingers again. The chauffeur in black, who had silently appeared behind them, stepped forward.

'I *am* a billionaire, aren't I, Hickson?'

'Yes, Sir John. Many times.'

'Thought so. And I think I own some island somewhere. What was it called now . . . Tasmania, I think.'

Wobbler patted his pockets again, and finally brought out a slim silver case. He flicked it open and took out two white pills, which he swallowed. He grimaced, and sipped from his glass of water.

'You haven't touched your One with Everything,' said Johnny, watching him.

'Oh, I asked for it just to make the point,' said Wobbler. 'I'm not allowed to eat them. Good heavens. I have a diet. No sodium, no cholesterol, low starch, no sugar.' He sighed. 'Even a glass of water is probably too exciting.'

The manager of the burger bar had at last plucked up the courage to approach the table.

'Sir John!' he said, 'This is a such an honour—'

'Yes, yes, thank you, please go away, I'm talking to my friends—' Wobbler stopped, and smiled evilly. 'Fries all right, Bigmac? Properly crisp?' he said. 'What about that milkshake, Yo-less? Right sort of texture, is it?'

The boys glanced up at the manager, who suddenly looked like a man praying to the god of everyone who has to work while wearing a name-badge saying 'My name is KEITH'.

'Er . . . they're fine,' said Bigmac.

'Great,' said Yo-less.

KEITH gave them a relieved grin.

'They're always good,' said Yo-less.

'I expect', said Bigmac, 'that they'll go *on* being good.'

KEITH nodded hurriedly.

'We're gen'rally in most Saturdays,' added Bigmac, helpfully. 'If you want us to make sure.'

'Thank you, Keith, you may go,' said Wobbler. He winked at Bigmac as the man almost ran away.

'I know I shouldn't do it,' he said, 'but it's about the only fun I get these days.'

'Why did you come here?' said Johnny quietly.

'You know, I couldn't resist doing a *little* checking,' said Wobbler, ignoring him. 'I thought it might be . . . interesting . . . to watch myself growing up. Not interfering, of course.' He stopped smiling. 'And then I found I wasn't born. I'd never been born. Nor was my father. My mother lived in London and was married to someone else. That's one thing about money. You can buy any amount of private detectives.'

'That's nonsense,' said Kirsty. 'You're *alive*.'

'Oh, yes,' said Wobbler. 'I was born. In another time. In the leg of the trousers of time that we were all born in. And then I went back in time with you all, and . . . something went wrong. I'm not sure what. So . . . I had to come back the long way. You could say I had to walk home.'

'I'm sure that's not logical,' said Kirsty.

Wobbler shrugged. 'I don't think time is all that logical,' he said. 'It bends itself around humans. It's probably full of loose ends. Whoever said it shouldn't be? Sometimes loose ends are necessary. If they weren't, spaghetti would be merely an embarrassing experience.' He chuckled. 'Spoke to a lot of scientists about this. Damn fools. Idiots! Time's in our heads. Any fool can see that—'

'You're ill, aren't you,' said Johnny.

'Is it obvious?'

'You keep taking pills, and your breathing doesn't sound right.'

Wobbler smiled again. But this time there was no humour in it.

'I'm suffering from life,' he said. 'However, I'm nearly cured.'

'Look,' said Kirsty, in the voice of one who is trying to be reasonable against the odds, 'we weren't going to leave you there. We were going to go back. We *will* go back.'

'Good,' said Wobbler.

'You don't mind? Because surely, if we *do*, you won't exist, will you?'

'Oh, I will. Somewhere,' said Wobbler.

'That's right,' said Johnny. 'Everything that happens . . . stays happened. Somewhere. There's lots of times side by side.'

'You always were a bit of an odd thinker,' said Wobbler. 'I remember that. An imagination so big it's outside your head. Now . . . what was the other thing? Oh, yes. I think I have to give you this.'

The chauffeur stepped forward.

'Er . . . Sir John, you know the Board did want—'

There was a blur in the air. Wobbler's silver-headed cane hit the table so hard that Bigmac's fries flew into the air. The *crack* echoed around the restaurant.

'God damn it, man, I'm paying you, and you will do what I say! The Board can wait! I'm not dead *yet*! I didn't get where I am today by listening to a lot of lawyers whining! I'm having some time off! Go away!'

Wobbler reached into his jacket and took out an envelope. He handed it to Johnny.

'I'm not telling you to go back,' he said. 'I've got no right. I've had a pretty good life, one way and the other—'

'But,' said Johnny. Through the glass doors of the mall he could see a car and four motorcycles pull up.

'I'm sorry?' said Wobbler.

'The next word you were going to say was "but",' said Johnny. Men were hurrying up the steps.

'Oh, yes. But . . . ' Wobbler leaned forward, and began speaking quickly. 'If you go back, I've written a letter to . . . well, you'll know what to do with it. I know I really shouldn't do it, but who could pass up an opportunity like this?'

He stood up, or at least attempted to. Hickson rushed up as Wobbler caught the edge of his chair, but was waved away.

'I never had any children,' said Wobbler. 'Never got married. Don't know why, really. It just didn't seem right.'

He leaned heavily on his stick and turned back to them.

'I want to be young again,' he said. 'Somewhere.'

'We were going to go back,' said Johnny. 'Honestly.'

'Good. But, you see . . . it's not just a case of going back. It's going back and doing the right things.'

And then he was gone, walking heavily towards the men with the suits, who closed in behind him.

Bigmac was staring so much that a long rivulet of mustard, tomato sauce, special chilli relish and vivid green chutney had dripped out of his burger and down his sleeve without him noticing.

'Wow,' said Yo-less, under his breath. 'Will *we* be like that one day?'

'What? Old? Probably,' said Johnny.

'I just can't get my head around old Wobbler being old,' said Bigmac, sucking at his sleeve.

'We've got to go and get him,' said Johnny. 'We can't let him get . . . '

'Rich?' said Yo-less. 'I don't think we can do anything about the "old" bit.'

'If we bring him back, then he – the old one – won't exist here,' said Kirsty.

'No, he'll exist in *this* here, but not in the *other* here. I don't think he'll be existing anywhere for very long anyway,' said Johnny. 'Come on.'

'What's in the envelope?' said Kirsty, as they left.

Johnny was surprised. Usually she'd say something like 'Let's see what's in this, then,' while snatching it out of his hand.

'It's for Wobbler,' said Johnny.

'He's written a letter to *himself*? What's he say?'

'How do I know? I don't open other people's letters!'

Johnny shoved the envelope back into his inside pocket.

'The keep-fit club should have finished by now,' he said. 'Come on.'

'Wait,' said Kirsty. 'If we're going back to 1941, let's go *prepared* this time, shall we?'

'Yeah,' said Bigmac. 'Armed.'

'No. Properly dressed, I mean.'

9

'Every Little Girl . . .'

It was an hour later. They met behind the church, in the damp little yard where they'd left the trolley.

'All *right*,' said Kirsty. 'Where did you get that outfit, Johnny?'

'Grandad's got loads of stuff in the attic. These are his old football shorts. And he always wears old pullovers, so I thought that was probably OK, too. And I've got my project stuff in this box in case it helps. It's genuine 1940s. It's what they carried gasmasks in.'

'Oh, is *that* what they are?' said Bigmac. 'I *thought* people had rather big Walkmans.'

'At least take the cap off, you look like Just William,' said Kirsty. 'What's this, Yo-less?'

'Me and Bigmac went along to that theatre shop in Wallace Street,' said Yo-less. 'What do you think?' he added uncertainly.

He shuffled round nervously. He was wearing a broad-brimmed hat, shoes with soles like two bumper cars parked side by side, and tight trousers. At least, what could be seen of the trousers looked tight.

'Is that an overcoat?' said Johnny critically.

'It's called a drape jacket,' said Yo-less.

'Bright red,' said Kirsty. 'Yes, I can see no-one will notice you at all. And those trousers . . . you must have had to grease your feet to get them on.'

'It looks a bit . . . stylish,' said Johnny. 'You know . . . jazzy.'

'The man in the shop said it's about right for the period,' said Yo-less defensively.

'You look like you're about to play the saxophone,' said Johnny. 'I mean . . . well, I've never seen you looking so . . . you know . . . cool.'

'That's why it's a disguise,' said Yo-less.

Kirsty turned to Bigmac, and sighed.

'Bigmac, why is it I get this feeling you've missed the point?'

'I *told* him,' said Yo-less. 'But he wouldn't listen.'

'The man said they wore this in 1941,' said Bigmac defensively.

'Yes, but don't you think that people might notice it's a *German* uniform?'

Bigmac looked panicky.

'Is it? I thought Yo-less was trying to wind me up! I thought they had all swastikas and stuff!'

'That's the Gestapo. You're dressed up like an ordinary German soldier.'

'I can't help it, it's the only one they had left, it was this or chain mail!'

'At least leave the jacket and helmet off, all right? Then it'll probably look like any other uniform.'

'Why're you wearing that fur coat, Kirsty?' said Johnny. 'You always say that wearing the skins of dead animals is murder.'

160

'Yeah, but she only says it to old ladies in fur coats,' muttered Bigmac under his breath. 'Bet she never says it to Hell's Angels in leather jackets.'

'*I* took some care,' said Kirsty, ignoring him. She adjusted her hat and shoulder bag. 'This is pretty accurate.'

'What, even the shoulders?'

'Yes. Shoulders were being worn wide.'

'Do you have to go through doors sideways?' said Yo-less.

'Let's get on with it, shall we?'

'What's worrying me is when old Wobb . . . I mean, *old* old Wobbler . . . said we've got to do the right things to bring him back,' said Yo-less. 'What things?'

'We'll have to find out,' said Johnny. 'He didn't say it was easy.'

'Come on,' said Bigmac, opening the door. 'I miss old Wobbler.'

'Why?' said Kirsty.

''Cos I don't throw straight.'

The keep-fit people had long ago staggered home. Johnny shoved the trolley into the middle of the floor, and stared at the sacks. Guilty was still asleep on a couple of them.

'Er . . . ' said Yo-less. 'This isn't *magic*, is it?'

'I don't think so,' said Johnny. 'It's probably just very, very, very strange science.'

'Oh, good,' said Yo-less. 'Er . . . what's the difference?'

'Who cares?' said Kirsty. 'Get on with it.'

Guilty started to purr.

Johnny picked up a bag. It seemed to wriggle in his grasp. With great care, he loosened the string.

And concentrated.

It was easier this time. Before, he'd just been dragged along like a cork in a current. This time he knew where he was going. He could *feel* the time.

Minds moved in time all the time. All the sacks did was let your body come too, just like Mrs Tachyon had said.

Years spiralled into the bag like water down a plughole. Time sucked out of the room.

And then there were the pews, and the scent of highly-polished holiness.

And Wobbler, turning around with his mouth open.

'*What—?*'

'It's all right, it's us,' said Johnny.

'Are you all right?' said Yo-less.

Wobbler might not have been the winner of the All-Europe Uptake Speed Trials, but an expression of deep suspicion spread across his face as he looked at them.

'What's up?' he said. 'You're all looking at me as if I'd gone weird! And what're you all dressed up for? Why's Bigmac wearing a German uniform?'

'See?' said Yo-less triumphantly. 'I *said* so, and does anyone listen?'

'We've just come back to fetch you,' said Johnny. 'There's no problem.'

'That's right. No problem at all,' said Yo-less. 'Everything's fine.'

'Yeah, fine. Everything's fine,' said Bigmac. 'Er . . . you're not feeling . . . *old*, are you?'

'What? After five minutes?' said Wobbler.

'I've brung you something,' said Bigmac. He took a square, flat shape from his pocket. It was rather battered, but it was nevertheless the only styrofoam box currently existing on the planet.

It was a BigWob . . . One with Everything.

'Did you nick that?' said Yo-less.

'Well, the old bloke said he wasn't going to eat it,' said Bigmac. 'So it'd only get chucked away, all right? It's not stealing if it'd only get chucked away. Anyway, it *is* his, isn't it, because—'

'You're not going to *eat* that, are you?' said Kirsty quickly. 'It's cold and greasy and it's been in Bigmac's pocket, for heaven's sake.'

Wobbler lifted out the bun.

'I could eat it even if a giraffe'd licked it,' he said, and bit into the cold bread. 'Hey, this isn't bad! Whose is it?' He looked at the face printed on the box. 'Who's the old fart with the beard?'

'Just some old fart,' said Johnny.

'Yeah, we don't know anything about him at all,' said Bigmac.

Wobbler gave them a suspicious look.

'What's going on here?' he said.

'Look, I can't explain now,' said Johnny. 'You're . . . stuck here. Er. Apparently, er, something's gone wrong. Er. There's been a snag.'

'What kind of snag?'

'Er. Quite a big one.'

Wobbler stopped eating. It was *that* serious.

'How big?' he said.

'Er. You're not going to be born . . . er.'

Wobbler stared at him. Then he stared at the half-eaten burger.

'Am I eating this burger? Are these my teeth marks?' he demanded.

'Look, it's perfectly *simple*,' said Kirsty. 'You're alive here, yes, but when we first came back, something must have happened which changed history. Everything anyone does changes history. So there's two histories. You were born in one, but things have been changed and when we got back it was into a different history where you weren't. All we have to do is put things back the way they should be, and then everything will be all right.'

'Hah! You haven't got a shelf of Star Trek videos as well, have you?' said Wobbler.

Kirsty looked as though someone had hit her.

'Well, er, I don't, er, what?' she said. 'Er . . . one or two . . . a few . . . not many . . . so what, anyway? I hardly ever look at them!'

'Hey,' said Yo-less, brightening up, 'have you got that one where a mysterious force—'

'Just shut up! Just shut up right now! Just because the programme happens to be an accurate reflection of late 20th century social concerns, *actually*, it doesn't mean you can go around winding people up just because they've

164

been taking an academic interest!'

'Have you got a Star Trek uniform?' said Yo-less.

Kirsty started to go red.

'If any of you tell *anybody* else there'll be big trouble,' said Kirsty. 'I mean it!'

Johnny opened the door of the church. Outside, Wednesday afternoon was turning into Wednesday evening. It was raining gently. He took a deep breath of 1941 air. It smelled of coal and pickles and jam, with a hint of hot rubber. People were *making* things. All those chimneys . . .

No-one made anything in Blackbury in 1996. There was a factory that put together computers, and some big warehouses, and the Department of Road Signs regional headquarters. People just moved things around, or added up numbers.

'So I watch some science fiction films,' said a plaintive voice behind him. 'At least I do it in a spirit of intelligent deconstruction. I don't just sit there saying "Cor, lasers, brill!"'

'No-one said you did,' said Yo-less, managing to sound infuriatingly reasonable.

'You're not going to let me forget this, are you?' said Kirsty.

'Won't mention it ever again,' said Yo-less.

'If we do, may we be pulled apart by wild Vegans,' said Bigmac, smirking.

'No, vegans are the people who don't eat animal products,' said Yo-less. 'You mean Vulcans. Vulcans are the ones with green blood—'

'Will you lot shut up? Here's me not even being

born and you're goin' on about daft aliens!' said Wobbler.

'What did we do here that changed the future?' said Johnny, turning around.

'Practically everything, I suppose,' said Kirsty. 'And Bigmac left all his stuff at the police station.'

'They shot at me—'

'Let's face it,' said Yo-less, '*anything* we do changes the future. Maybe we bumped into someone so he was five seconds late crossing the road and got hit by a car or something. Like treading on a dinosaur. Any little thing changes the whole of history.'

'That's daft,' said Bigmac. 'I mean, rivers still flow the same way no matter how the little fish swim.'

'Er . . . ' said Wobbler. 'There was this . . . kid . . .'

He said it in the slow, plonking tones of someone who is afraid that he might have come up with an important piece of evidence.

'What kid?' said Johnny.

'Just some kid,' said Wobbler. 'He was running away from home or something. *To* home, I mean. All long shorts and bogeys up the nose.'

'What do you mean, running to home?'

'Oh, he was goin' on about being evacuated here and being fed up and running off back to London. But he followed me back into town throwing stones at me 'cos he said I was a spy. He's probably still outside, 's'matter of fact. He ran off down that road there.'

'Paradise Street?' said Johnny.

166

'What about it?' said Wobbler, looking worried.

'It's going to be bombed tonight,' said Kirsty. 'Johnny's got a thing about it.'

'Hah, can't see any Germans wanting to bomb *him*, he was practically on their side,' said Wobbler.

'Are you sure it was Paradise Street?' said Johnny. 'Are you *sure*? Did you have any relatives there? Grandparents? *Great*-grandparents?'

'How should I know? That was ages ago!'

Johnny took a deep breath. 'It's right now!'

'I-I-I don't know! One of my grandads lives in Spain and the other one died before I was born!'

'How?' said Kirsty.

'Fell off a motorbike, I think. In 1971.' Wobbler brightened up. 'See? So that's all right.'

'Oh, Wobbler, Wobbler, it's *not* all right!' said Johnny. 'Get it into your head! Where did he live?'

Wobbler was trembling, as he always did when life was getting too exciting.

'I dunno! London, I think! My dad said he came up here in the war! And then later on he came back on a visit and met my grandma! Er! Er!'

'Go on! Go on!' said Johnny.

'Er! Er!' Wobbler stuttered.

'How old was he when he died?' said Yo-less.

'Er! Forty, my dad said! Er! He'd bought the bike for his birthday!'

'So he's . . . ' Johnny subtracted in his head, ' . . . ten now?'

'Er! Er!'

'You don't think he was that boy, do you?' said Yo-less.

'Oh, yes,' said Wobbler, finally giving up panic for anger. 'I should have asked him, should I? "Hello, are you going to be my grandad? PS don't buy a motorbike"?'

Johnny fished in his gas mask box and pulled out a crumpled folder stuffed with bits of paper.

'Did he mention any names?' he said, flicking through the pages.

'Er! Er! Someone called Mrs Density!' said Wobbler, desperation throwing up a memory.

'Number Eleven,' said Johnny, pulling out a photocopy of a newspaper clipping. 'Lived there with her daughter Gladys. I got all the names for my project.'

'My gran's name was Gladys!' said Wobbler. 'You mean, because he *didn't* run off back to London, he's going to die tonight and I'm not going to be born?'

'Could be,' said Yo-less.

'What'll happen to me?'

'You'll just have to stay here,' said Johnny.

'No way! This is the *olden days*! It's awful! I went past a cinema and it's all old movies! In black and white! And there was this cafe and you know what they'd got chalked on a board in front? "Meat and two veg"! What kind of food is that? Even Hong Kong Henry's takeaway tells you what *kind* of meat! Everyone dresses like someone out of Eastern Europe! I'd go round the bend here!'

'*My* grandad always goes on about how they used to have so much fun when he was a kid even though they didn't have anything,' said Bigmac.

'Yes, but everyone's grandad says that,' said Kirsty. 'It's compulsory. It's like where they say "50p for a chocolate bar? When I was young you could get one and still have change out of sixpence."'

'I think they had fun,' said Johnny, 'because they didn't *know* they didn't have anything.'

'Well, *I* know,' said Wobbler. 'I know about food that's more than two colours, and stereo systems, and decent music and . . . and all kinds of stuff! I want to go *home*!'

They all looked at Johnny.

'You got us into this,' said Yo-less.

'Me?'

'It's your imagination,' said Kirsty. 'It's too big for your head, just like Sir J . . . ' She stopped. 'Just like I've always said,' she corrected herself, 'and it drags everyone else along with it. I don't know how, but it does. You got all worked up about Paradise Street, and now here we are.'

'You said it didn't make any difference if the street got bombed or not,' said Johnny. '*You* said it was just history!'

'*I* don't want to be history!' moaned Wobbler.

'All *right*, you win,' said Kirsty. 'What do you want us to do?'

Johnny shuffled the papers.

'Well . . . what I found out for my project was

169

that . . . there was a big storm, you see. The weather got very bad. And the bombers must've seen Blackbury and dropped their bombs *anyway* and turned around. That used to happen. There was . . . there *is* an air-raid siren. It was supposed to go off if bombers were near,' he said. 'Only it didn't.'

'Why not?'

The folder shut with a snap.

'Let's start by finding out,' said Johnny.

It was on a pole on the roof in the High Street. It didn't look very big.

'That's all it is?' said Yo-less. 'Looks like a giant yo-yo.'

'That's an air-raid siren all right,' said Kirsty. 'I saw a picture in a book.'

'How d'they work? Set off by radar or something?'

'I'm sure that's not been invented yet,' said Johnny.

'Well, how then?'

'Maybe there's a switch somewhere?'

'It'd be somewhere safe, then,' said Yo-less. 'Somewhere where people wouldn't be able to set it off for a laugh.'

Their joint gaze travelled down the pole, across the roof, down the wall, past the blue lamp, and stopped when it met the words: 'Police Station'.

'Oh, dear,' said Yo-less.

They sat down on a bench by a civic flower-bed, opposite the door. A policeman came out and stood in the sunshine, watching them back.

'It's a good job we left Bigmac to guard the trolley,' said Yo-less.

'Yes,' said Johnny. 'He's always been allergic to policemen.'

Kirsty sighed. 'Honestly, you boys haven't got a clue.'

She stood up, crossed the road and began to talk to the policeman. They could hear the conversation. It went like this:

'Excuse me, officer—'

He gave her a friendly smile.

'Yes, little lady? Out in your mum's clothes, are you?'

Kirsty's eyes narrowed.

'Oh, dear,' said Johnny, under his breath.

'What's the matter?' said Yo-less.

'Well, you know you and "Sambo"? That's Kirsty and words like "little lady".'

'I was just wondering', said the little lady, through clenched teeth, 'how that big siren works.'

'Oh, I shouldn't worry your head about that, love,' said the policeman. 'It's very complicated. You wouldn't understand.'

'Look for something to hide behind,' said Johnny. 'Like another planet.'

Then his mouth dropped open as Kirsty won a medal.

'It's just that I get *so* worried,' she said, and managed a simper, or what she probably thought was a simper. 'I'm *sure* Mr Hitler's bombers are going to come one night and the siren won't go off. I can't get to sleep for worrying!'

The policeman laid a hand on the shoulder of the girl who had left Blackbury Karate Club because no boy would dare come within two metres of her.

'Oh, we can't have that, love,' he said. He pointed. 'See up there on Blackdown? Well, Mr Hodder and his very brave men are up there every night, keeping a look-out. If any planes come near here tonight he'll ring the station in a brace of shakes, don't you worry.'

'But supposing the phone doesn't work?'

'Oh, then he'll be down here on his bike in no time.'

'Bike? A bike? That's *all*?'

'It's a *motor*bike,' said the policeman, giving her the nervous looks everyone eventually gave Kirsty.

She just stared at him.

'It's a Blackbury Phantom,' he added still further, in a tone of voice that suggested this should impress even a girl.

'Oh? Really? Oh, that's a relief,' said Kirsty. 'I feel a lot better for knowing that. Really.'

'That's right. There's nothing for you to worry about, love,' said the policeman happily.

'I'll just go off and play with my dolls, I expect,' said Kirsty.

'That's a good idea. Have a tea party,' said the policeman, who apparently didn't know withering scorn when he heard it.

Kirsty crossed the road and sat down on the seat.

'Yes, I expect I should have a party with all my dollies,' she said, glaring at the flowers.

Yo-less looked at Johnny over her head.

'What?' he said.

'Did you hear what that ridiculous policeman said?' said Kirsty. 'Honestly, it's obvious that the stupid man thinks that just because I'm female I've got the brains of a baby. I mean, good grief! Imagine living in a time when people could even *think* like that without being prosecuted!'

'Imagine living in a time when a bomb could come through your ceiling,' said Johnny.

'Mind you, my father said he lived in the shadow of the atomic bomb all through the Sixties,' said Kirsty. 'I think that was why he wore flares. Hah! Dollies! Pink dresses and pink ribbons. "Don't worry your head about that, girlie." This is the *dark ages.*'

Yo-less patted her on the arm.

'He didn't mean it . . . you know, nastily,' he said. 'It's just how he was brought up. You people can't expect us to rewrite history, you know—'

Kirsty frowned at him.

'Is that sarcasm?' she said.

'Who? Me?' said Yo-less innocently.

'All right, all right, you've made your point. What's so special about a Blackbury Phantom, anyway?'

'They used to make them here,' said Johnny. 'They were quite famous, I think. Grandad used to have one.'

They raised their eyes to the dark shape of Blackdown. It had loomed over the town even back in 1996, but then it had a TV mast.

'That's *it*?' said Kirsty. 'Men just sitting on hills and listening?'

'Well, Blackbury wasn't very important,' said Johnny. 'We made jam and pickles and rubber boots and that was about it.'

'I wonder what's going to go wrong tonight?' said Yo-less.

'We could climb up there and find out,' said Johnny. 'Let's go and get the others—'

'Hang on,' said Kirsty. '*Think*, will you? How do you know we might not *cause* what's going to go wrong tonight?'

Johnny hesitated. For a moment he looked like a statue. Then he said:

'No. If we start thinking like that we'll never do anything.'

'We've already messed up the future once! *Everything* we do affects the future!'

'It always has. It always will. So what? Let's get the others.'

10

Running Into Time

There was no question of using the roads, not with the police still looking for a Bigmac who, with a wardrobe of costumes to chose from, had chosen to go back in time wearing a German soldier's uniform.

They'd have to use the fields and footpaths. Which meant—

'We'll have to leave the trolley,' said Yo-less. 'We can shove it in the bushes here.'

'That means we'll be stuck here if anything goes wrong!' said Bigmac.

'Well, I'm not lugging it through mud and stuff.'

'What if someone finds it?'

'There's Guilty,' said Kirsty. 'He's better than a guard dog.'

The cat that was better than a guard dog opened one eye and yawned. It was true. No-one would want to be bitten by that mouth. It would be like being savaged by a plague laboratory.

Then he curled into a more comfortable ball.

'Yes, but it belongs to Mrs Tachyon,' said Johnny, weakly.

'Hey, we're not thinking sensibly – again,' said Kirsty. 'All we have to do is go back to 1996, go up to Blackdown on the bus, then come back in time again and we'll be up there—'

'No!' shouted Wobbler.

His face was bright red with terror.

'I'm not stopping here by myself again! I'm stuck here, remember? Supposing you don't come back?'

'Of course we'll come back,' said Johnny. 'We came back this time, didn't we?'

'Yes, but supposing you don't? Supposing you get run over by a lorry or something? What'll happen to me?'

Johnny thought about the long envelope in his inside pocket. Yo-less and Bigmac were looking at their feet. Even Kirsty was looking away.

'Here,' said Wobbler suspiciously. 'This is time travel, right? Do you know something horrible?'

'We don't know anything,' said Bigmac.

'Absolutely right,' said Kirsty.

'What, us? We don't know a thing,' said Johnny miserably.

'Especially about burgers,' said Bigmac.

Kirsty groaned. '*Bigmac!*'

Wobbler glared at them.

'Oh, yes,' he muttered. 'It's "wind up ole Wobbler" time again, right? Well, I'm going to stay with the trolley, right? It's not going anywhere without me, right?'

He stared from one to the other, daring them to disagree.

'All right, I'll stay with you,' said Bigmac. 'I'll probably only get shot anyway, if I go anywhere.'

'What're you going to do up on Blackdown, anyway?' said Wobbler. 'Find this Mr Hodder and tell him to listen really carefully? Wash out his ears? Eat plenty of carrots?'

'They're for good eyesight,' said Yo-less helpfully. 'My granny said they used to believe carrots helped you see in—'

'Who cares!'

'I don't know *what* we can do,' said Johnny. 'But . . . something must have gone wrong, right? Maybe the message didn't get through. We'll have to make sure it does.'

'Look,' said Kirsty.

The sun had already set, leaving an afterglow in the sky. And there were clouds over Blackdown. Dark clouds.

'Thunderstorm,' she said. 'They always start up there.'

There was a growl in the distance.

Blackbury was a lot smaller once they were in the hills. A lot of it wasn't there at all.

'Wouldn't it be great if we could tell everyone what they're going to do wrong,' said Johnny, when they paused for breath.

'No-one'd listen,' said Yo-less. 'Supposing someone turned up in 1996 and said they were from 2040 and started telling everyone what to do? They'd get arrested, wouldn't they?'

Johnny looked ahead of them. The sunset sky lurked behind bars of angry cloud.

'The listeners'll be up at the Tumps,' said Kirsty. 'There's an old windmill up there. It was some kind of look-out post during the war. Is, I mean.'

'Why didn't you say so before?' said Johnny.

'It's different when it's now.'

The Tumps were five mounds on top of the down. They grew heather and wortleberries. It was said that dead kings were buried there in the days when your enemy was at arm's length rather than ten thousand feet above your head.

The clouds were getting lower. It was going to be one of those Blackbury storms, a sort of angry fog that hugged the hills.

'You know what I'm thinking?' said Kirsty.

'Telephone lines,' said Johnny. 'They go out in thunderstorms.'

'Right.'

'But the policeman said there was a motorbike,' said Yo-less.

'Starts first time, does it?' said Johnny. 'I remember my grandad said that before you were qualified to ride a Blackbury Phantom you had to learn to push it fifty metres, cursing all the way. He said they were great bikes when they got started.'

'How long is it till . . . you know . . . the bombs?'

'About an hour.'

Which means they're already on the way, Johnny thought. Men have walked out onto airfields and loaded bombs onto planes with names like Dorniers and Heinkels. And other men have sat round in front of a big map of England, only it'd be in

German, and there'd be crayon marks around Slate. Blackbury probably wasn't even on the map. And then they'd get up and walk out and get into the planes and take off. And men on the planes would get out *their* maps and draw lines on them; lines which crossed at Slate. Your mission for tonight: bomb the goods yard at Slate.

And then the roar filled his ears. The drone of the engines came up through his legs. He could taste the oil and the sweat and the stale rubber smell of the oxygen mask. His body shook with the throb of the engines and also with the thump of distant explosions. One was very close and the whole aircraft seemed to slide sideways. And he knew what the mission for tonight was. Your mission for tonight is *to get home safely*. It always was.

Another explosion shook the plane, and someone grabbed him.

'What?'

'It's weird when you do that!' shouted Kirsty, above the thunder. 'Come on! It's *dangerous* out here! Haven't you got enough sense to get out of the rain?'

'It's starting to happen,' Johnny whispered, while the storm broke around him.

'What is?'

'The future!'

He blinked as the rain started to plaster his hair against his head. He could *feel* time stretching out around him. He could feel its slow movement as it carried forward all those grey bombs and those white doorsteps, pulling them together like bubbles being swirled around a whirlpool. They were all carried along by it. You couldn't break out of it because you were *part* of it. You couldn't steer a train.

'We'd better get him under cover!' shouted Yo-less as lightning hit something a little way off. 'He doesn't look well at *all*!'

They staggered on, occasionally lurking under a wind-bent tree to get their breath back.

There was a windmill among the Tumps. It had been built on one of the mounds, although the sails had long gone. The others put their arms around Johnny and ran through the soaking heather until they reached it and climbed the steps.

Yo-less hammered on the door. It opened a fraction.

'Good lord!' said a voice. It sounded like the voice of a young man. 'What're you? A circus?'

'You've got to let us in!' said Kirsty. 'He's ill!'

'Can't do that,' said the voice. 'Not allowed, see?'

'Do we look like spies?' shouted Yo-less.

'Please!' said Kirsty.

The door started to close, and then stopped.

'Well . . . all right,' said the voice, as unseen hands pulled the door open. 'But Mr Hodder says to stand where we can see you, OK? Come on in.'

'It's happening,' said Johnny, who still had his eyes closed. 'The telephone won't work.'

'What's he going on about?'

'Can you try the telephone?' said Kirsty.

'Why? What's wrong with it?' said the boy. 'We tested it out at the beginning of the shift just now. Has anyone been mucking about with it?'

There was an older man sitting at a table. He gave them a suspicious look, which lingered for a while on Yo-less.

'I reckon you'd better try the station,' he said. 'I don't like the sound of all this. Seems altogether a bit suspicious to me.'

The first man reached out towards the phone.

There was a sound outside as lightning struck somewhere close. It wasn't a *zzzippp* – it was almost a gentle silken hiss, as the sky was cut in half.

Then the phone exploded. Bits of bakelite and copper clattered off the walls.

Kirsty's hand flew to her head.

'My hair stood on end!'

'So did mine,' said Yo-less. 'And that doesn't often happen, believe me,' he added.

'Lightning hit the wire,' said Johnny. 'I knew that. Not just here. Other stations on the hills, too. And now he'll have trouble with the motorbike.'

'What's he going on about?'

'You've got a motorbike, haven't you?' said Kirsty.

'So what?'

'Good grief, man, you've lost your telephone! Aren't you supposed to do something about that?'

The men looked at one another. Girls weren't supposed to shout like Kirsty.

'Tom, nip down to Doctor Atkinson's and use his phone and tell the station ours has gone for a burton,' said Mr Hodder, not taking his eyes off the three. 'Tell them about these kids, too.'

'It won't start,' said Johnny. 'It's the carburettor, I think. That . . . always gives trouble.'

The one called Tom looked at him sideways. There was a change in the air. Up until now the men had just been suspicious. Now they were uneasy, too.

'How did you know that?' he said.

Johnny opened his mouth. And shut it again.

He couldn't tell them about the feel of the *time* around him. He felt that if he could only focus his eyes properly, he could even see it. The past and future were there, just around some kind of corner, bound up to the ever-travelling *now* by a billion connections. He felt that he could almost reach out and point, not there or over there or up there but *there*, at right angles to everywhere else.

'They're on their way,' he said. 'They'll be here in half an hour.'

'What will? What's he going on about?'

'Blackbury's going to be bombed tonight,' said Kirsty. Thunder rolled again.

'We think,' said Yo-less.

'Five planes,' said Johnny.

He opened his eyes. Everything overlapped like a scene in a kaleidoscope. Everyone was staring at him, but they were surrounded by something like fog. When they moved, images followed them like some kind of special effect.

'It's the storm and the clouds,' he managed to say. 'They think they're going to Slate but they'll drop their bombs over Blackbury.'

'Oh, yes? And how d'you know this, then? They told you, did they?'

'Listen, you stupid man,' said Kirsty. 'We're not spies! Why would we *tell* you if we were?'

Mr Hodder pulled open the door.

'I'm going down to use the doctor's phone,' he said. 'Then maybe we can sort out what's going on.'

'What about the bombers?' said Kirsty.

The older man opened the door. The thunder had rolled away to the north-east, and there was no sound but the hiss of the rain.

'What bombers?' he said, and shut it behind him.

Johnny sat down with his head in his hands, blinking his eyes again to shut out the flickering images.

'You lot'd better get out,' said Tom. 'It's against the rules, having people in here . . . '

Johnny blinked. There were more bombers in front of his eyes, and they *didn't* go away.

He scrabbled at the playing cards on the table.

'What're these for?' he said urgently. 'Playing cards with bombers on them?'

'Eh? What? Oh . . . that's for learning aircraft recognition,' said Tom, who'd been careful to keep the table between him and Johnny. 'You plays cards with 'em and you sort of picks up the shapes, like.'

'You learn subliminally?' said Kirsty.

'Oh, no, you learn from playing with these here cards,' said Tom desperately. Outside, there was the sound of someone trying to start a motorbike.

Johnny stood up.

'All right,' he said. 'I can *prove* it. The next card . . . the next card you show me . . . the next card . . .'

Images filled his eyes. If this is how Mrs Tachyon sees the world, he thought, no wonder she never seems all there – because she's *everywhere*.

Outside, there was the sound of someone trying to start a motorbike even harder.

' . . . the next card . . . will be the five of diamonds.'

'I don't see why I should have to play games—' The man glanced nervously at Kirsty, who had that effect on people.

'Scared?' she said.

He grabbed a card at random and held it up.

'It's the five of diamonds all right,' said Yo-less.

Johnny nodded. 'The next one . . . the next one . . . the next one will be the knave of hearts.'

It was.

Outside, there was the sound of someone trying to start a motorbike very hard and swearing.

'It's a trick,' said the man. 'One of you messed around with the pack.'

'Shuffle them all you like,' said Johnny. 'And the next one you show me will be . . . the ten of clubs.'

'How did you do that?' said Yo-less, as the boy turned the card over and stared at it.

'Er . . .' It had *felt* like memory, he told himself. 'I remembered seeing it,' said Johnny.

'You remembered seeing it before you actually saw it?' said Kirsty.

Outside, there was the sound of someone trying to start a motorbike very hard and swearing even harder.

'Er . . . yes.'

'Oh, wow,' she said. 'Precognition. You're probably a natural medium.'

'Er, I'm a size eleven,' said Johnny, but they weren't listening.

Kirsty had turned to Tom.

'You see?' she said. 'Now do you believe us?'

'I don't like this. This isn't right,' he said. 'Anyway . . . anyway, there's no phone—'

The door burst open.

'All right!' roared Mr Hodder. 'What did you kids do to my bike?'

'It's the carburettor,' said Johnny. 'I told you.'

'Here, Arthur, you ought to listen to this, this boy knows things—'

Kirsty glanced at her watch.

'Twenty minutes,' she said. 'It's more than two miles down to the town. Even if we ran I'm not sure we could do it.'

'What're you talking about now?' said Mr Hodder.

'There must be some kind of code,' said Kirsty. 'If you have to ring up and tell them to sound the siren, what do you say?'

'Don't tell them!' snapped Mr Hodder.

'"This is station BD3",' said Johnny, his eyes looking unfocused.

'How did you know that? Did he tell you? Did you tell them?'

'No, Arthur!'

'Come on,' said Kirsty, hurrying towards the door. 'I got a county medal in athletics!'

She elbowed the older man aside.

The thunder was growling away in the east. The storm had settled down to a steady, grey rain.

'We'll never make it,' said Yo-less.

'I thought you people were good at running,' said Kirsty, stepping out.

'People of my height, you mean?'

'You were right,' said the young man, as Johnny was dragged out into the night. 'This *is* station BD3!'

'I know,' said Johnny. 'I remembered you just telling me.'

He staggered and grabbed at Yo-less to stay upright. The world was spinning around him. He hadn't felt like this since that business with the cider at Christmas. The voices around him seemed to be muffled, and he couldn't be sure whether they were really there, or voices he was re-membering, or words that hadn't even been spoken yet.

He felt that his mind was being shaken loose in time, and it was only still here because his body was a huge great anchor.

'It's downhill all the way,' said Kirsty, and sped off. Yo-less followed her.

Far away, down in the town, a church clock began to strike eleven.

Johnny tried to lumber into a run, but the ground kept shifting under his feet.

Why are we doing this? he thought. We *know* it happened, I've got a copy of the paper in my pocket, the bombs *will* land and the siren *won't* go off.

You can't steer a train!

That's what *you* think, said a voice in his head . . .

He wished he'd been better at this. He wished he'd been a hero.

From up ahead, he heard Yo-less's desperate cry.

'I've tripped over a sheep! I've tripped over a sheep!'

The lights of Blackbury spread out below them. There weren't many of them – the occasional smudge from a car, the tiny gleam from a window where the moths had got at the blackout curtain.

A wind had followed the storm. Streamers of cloud blew across the sky. Here and there a star shone through.

They ran on. Yo-less ran into another sheep in the blackness.

There was the crunch of heavy boots on the road behind them and Tom caught them up.

'If you're wrong there's going to be big trouble!' he panted.

'What if we're right?' said Kirsty.

'I hope you're wrong!'

Thunder rumbled again, but the four runners plunged on in a bubble of desperate silence.

They were leaving the moor behind. There were hedges on either side of the road now.

Tom's boots skidded to a halt.

'Listen!'

They stopped. There was the grumbling of the thunder and the hiss of the rain.

And, behind the noises of the weather, a faint and distant droning.

Gravel flew up as the young man started to run again. He'd been moving fast before but now he flew down the road.

A large house loomed up against the night. He leapt over the fence, pounded across the lawns, and started to hammer on the front door.

'Open up! Open up! It's an emergency!'

Johnny and the others reached the gate. The droning was louder now.

We could have done something, Johnny thought. *I* could have done something. I could've . . . well, there *must* have been *something*. We thought it would be so easy. Just because we're from the future. What do we know about anything? And now the bombers are nearly here and there's nothing we can do.

'Come on! Open up!'

Yo-less found a gate and hurried through it. There was a splash in the darkness.

'I think I've stepped into some sort of pond,' said a damp voice.

Tom stepped away from the house and groped on the ground for something.

'Maybe I can smash a window,' he mumbled.

'Er . . . it's quite deep,' said Yo-less, damply. 'And I'm caught up on some kind of fountain thing . . .'

Glass tinkled. Tom reached through the window beside the door. There was a click, and the door opened.

They heard him trip over something inside, and then a weak light went on. Another click and—

'This phone's dead too! The lightning must've got the exchange!'

'Where's the next house?' said Kirsty, as Tom hurtled down the path.

'Not till Roberts Road!'

They ran after him, Yo-less squelching slightly.

The drone was much louder now. Johnny could hear it above the sound of his own breath.

Someone *must* notice it in the town, he thought. It fills the whole sky!

Without saying anything, they all began to run faster—

And, at last, the siren began to wail.

But the clouds were parting and the moon shone through and there were shadows nosing through the rags of cloud and Johnny could feel the unseen shapes turning over and over as they drifted towards the ground.

First there was the allotment, and then the pickle factory, and then Paradise Street exploded gently, like a row of roses opening. The petals were orange tinged with black and unfolded one after another, as the bombs fell along the street.

Then the sounds arrived. They weren't bangs but crunches, punches, great wads of noise hammered into the head.

Finally they died away, leaving only a distant crackling and the rising sound of a fire bell.

'Oh, no!' said Kirsty.

Tom had stopped. He stood and stared at the distant flames.

'The phone wasn't working,' he whispered. 'I tried to get here but the phone wasn't working.'

'We're *time* travellers!' said Yo-less. 'This *isn't* supposed to happen!'

Johnny swayed slightly. The feeling was like flu, but much worse. He felt as if he were outside his own body, watching himself.

It was the *hereness* of here, the *nowness* of now . . . People survived by not paying any attention to feelings like this. If you stopped, and opened your head to them, the world would roll over you like a tank . . .

Paradise Street was always going to be bombed. It was being bombed. It would *have been* bombed. Tonight was a fossil in time. It was a *thing*. Somewhere, it would always have happened. You couldn't steer a train!

That's what you *think* . . .

Somewhere . . .

Flames flickered over the housetops. More bells were ringing.

'The bike wouldn't start!' mumbled Tom. 'The phone wouldn't work! There was a storm! I tried to get down here in time! How could it have been my fault?'

Somewhere . . .

Johnny felt it again . . . the sense that he could reach out and go in directions not found on any map or compass but only on a clock. It poured up from inside him until he felt that it was leaking out of his fingers. He hadn't got the trolley or the bags but . . . maybe he could remember how it felt . . .

'We've got time,' he said.

'Are you *mad*?' said Kirsty.

'Are you going to come or not?' said Johnny.

'Where?'

Johnny took her hand, and reached out for Yo-less with his other hand.

Then he nodded towards Tom, who was still staring at the flames.

'Grab him, too,' he said. 'We'll need him when we get there.'

'Where?'

Johnny tried to grin.

'Trust me,' he said. 'Someone has to.'

He started to walk. Tom was dragged along with them like a sleepwalker.

'Faster,' said Johnny. 'Or we'll never get there.'

'Look, the bombs have *fallen*,' said Kirsty, wearily. 'It's happened.'

'Right. It had to,' said Johnny. 'Otherwise we couldn't get there before it did. Faster. Run.'

He pushed forward, dragging them after him.

'I suppose we might be able to . . . help,' panted Yo-less. 'I know . . . first aid.'

'*First* aid?' said Kirsty. 'You saw the explosions!'

Beside her, the young man suddenly seemed to wake up. He stared at the fire in the town and lurched forward. And then they were all running, all trying to keep up, all causing the others to go faster.

And there was *the* road, in *that* direction.

Johnny took it.

The dark landscape lit up in shades of grey, like a very old film. The sky went from black to an inky purple. And everything around them looked cold, like crystal; all the leaves and bushes glittering as if they were covered in frost.

He couldn't *feel* cold. He couldn't feel anything.

Johnny ran. The road under his feet was sticky, as though he was trying to sprint in treacle.

And the air filled with the noise he'd last heard from the bags, a great whispering rush of sound, like a million radio stations slightly out of tune.

Beside him Yo-less tried to say something, but no words came out. He pointed with his free hand, instead.

Blackbury lay ahead of them. It wasn't the town

he knew in 1996, and it wasn't the one from 1941 either. It glowed.

Johnny had never seen the Northern Lights. He'd read about them, though. The book said that on very cold nights sometimes the lights would come marching down from the North Pole, hanging in the sky like curtains of frozen blue fire.

That was how the town looked. It gleamed, as cold as starlight on a winter night.

He risked a glance behind.

There, the sky was red, a deep crimson that brightened to a ruby glow at its centre.

And he knew that if he stopped running it would all end. The road would be a road again, the sky would be the sky . . . but if he just kept going in *this* direction . . .

He forced his legs to move onward, pedalling in slow motion through the thick, cold, silent air. The town got closer, brighter.

Now the others were pulling on his arms. Kirsty was trying to shout too, but there was no sound here except the roar of all the tiny noises.

He snatched at their fingers, trying to hold on . . .

And then the blue rushed towards him and met the red coming the other way and he was toppling forward onto the road.

He heard Kirsty say, 'I'm covered in ice!'

Johnny pushed himself to his feet and stared at his own arms. Ice crackled and fell off his sleeves as he moved.

Yo-less looked white. Frost steamed off his face.

'What did we do? What did we *do*?' said Kirsty.

'Listen, will you?' said Yo-less. 'Listen!'

There was a whirring somewhere in the darkness, and a clock began to strike.

Johnny listened. They were on the edge of town. There was no traffic in the dark streets. But there were no fires, either. There was the muffled sound of laughter from a nearby pub, and the chink of glasses.

The clock went on striking. The last note died away. A cat yowled.

'Eleven o'clock?' said Kirsty. 'But we *heard* eleven o'clock when we . . . were . . . on the downs . . . '

She turned and stared at Johnny.

'*You* took us *back* in *time*?'

'Not . . . back, I think,' said Johnny. 'I think . . . behind. Outside. Around. Across. I don't know!'

Tom had managed to get to his knees. What they could see of his face in the dusk said that here was a man to whom too much had happened, and whose brain was floating loose.

'We've got seven minutes,' said Johnny.

'Huh?' said Tom.

'To get them to sound the siren!' shouted Kirsty.

'Huh? The bombs . . . I saw the fires . . . it wasn't my fault, the phone—'

'They didn't! But they will! Unless you do something! Right now! On your feet right now!' shouted Kirsty.

No-one could resist a voice like that. It went

right through the brain and gave its commands directly to the muscles. Tom rose like a lift.

'Good! Now *come on*!'

The police station was at the end of the street. They reached the door in a group and fought one another to get through it.

There was an office inside, with a counter running across it to separate the public from the forces of Law and Order. A policeman was standing behind it. He had been writing in a large book, but now he was looking up with his mouth open.

'Hello, Tom,' he said. 'What's going on?'

'You've got to sound the siren!' said Johnny.

'Right now!' said Kirsty.

The sergeant looked from one to the other and then at Yo-less, where his gaze lingered for a while. Then he turned and glanced at a man in military uniform who was sitting writing at a desk in the office. The sergeant was the sort of man who liked an audience if he thought he was going to be funny.

'Oh, yes?' he said. 'And why should I do that, then?'

'They're right, sergeant,' said Tom. 'You've got to do it! We . . . ran all the way!'

'What, off the down?' said the sergeant. 'That's two miles, that is. Sounds a bit fishy to me, young man. Been round the back of the pub again, have you? Hah . . . remember that Dornier 111 bomber you heard last week?' He turned and smirked at the officer again. 'A lorry on the Slate road, that was!'

Kirsty's patience, which in any case was only

visible with special scientific equipment, came to an end.

'Don't you patronize us, you ridiculous buffoon!' she screamed.

The sergeant went red and took a deep breath. Then it was let out suddenly.

'Hey, where do you think *you're* going?'

Tom had scrambled over the desk. The soldier stood up but was pushed out of the way.

The young man reached the switch, and pulled it down.

11

You Want Fries With That?

Wobbler and Bigmac skulked behind the church.

'They've been gone a long time,' said Bigmac.

'It's a long way up there,' said Wobbler.

'I bet something's happened. They've been shot or something.'

'Huh, I thought you *liked* guns,' said Wobbler.

'I don't mind guns. I don't like bullets,' said Bigmac. 'And I don't want to get stuck here with you!'

'We've got the time trolley,' said Wobbler. 'But do you know how to work it? I reckon you've got to be half mental like Johnny to work it. I don't want to end up fighting Romans or something.'

'You won't,' said Bigmac.

He froze as he realized what he'd said. Wobbler homed in.

'What do you mean, stuck here with you? What *does* happen if I don't go home?' he said. 'You lot went back to 1996. I wasn't there, right?'

'Oh, you don't want to know any stuff like that,' said Bigmac.

'Oh, yeah?'

★   ★   ★

'You come in here and act cheeky—' the sergeant began.

'Be quiet!' snapped Captain Harris, standing up. 'Why doesn't your siren work?'

'We tests it every Tuesday and Friday, reg'lar—' said the sergeant.

'There's a hole in the ceiling,' said Yo-less.

Tom stood looking at the switch. He was certain he'd done his bit. He wasn't sure how, but he'd done it. And things that should be happening next weren't happening.

'It wasn't my fault,' he mumbled.

'Your man fired a gun,' said the sergeant. 'We never did know where the bullet went.'

'We know now,' said the captain grimly. 'It's hit a wire somewhere.'

'There's got to be some other way,' said Johnny. 'It *mustn't* end like this! Not after everything! Look!'

He pulled a crumpled piece of paper out of his pocket and held it up.

'What's that?' said the captain.

'It's tomorrow's newspaper,' said Johnny. 'If the siren doesn't go off.'

The captain stared at it.

'Oh, trying to pull our leg, eh?' said the police sergeant nervously.

The captain turned his eyes from the paper to Johnny's wrist. He grabbed it.

'Where did you get this watch?' he snapped. 'I've seen one like it before! Where do you come from, boy?'

'Here,' said Johnny. 'Sort of. But not . . . now.'

There was a moment's silence. Then the captain nodded at the sergeant.

'Ring up the local newspaper, will you?' he said. 'It's a morning paper, isn't it? Someone should still be there.'

'You're not seriously—'

'Please do it.'

Seconds ticked by as the policeman huddled over the big black phone. He muttered a few words.

'I've got Mr Stickers, the chief compositor,' he said. 'He says they're just clearing the front page and what do we want?'

The captain glanced at the paper, and sniffed at it.

'Fish? Never mind . . . is there an advertisement for Johnson's Cocoa in the bottom left hand corner of the page? Don't stare. Ask him.'

There was some mumbling.

'He says yes, but—'

The captain turned the page over.

'On page two, is there a single column story headed "Fined 2/6d for Bike Offence"? On the crossword, is One Down "Bird of Stone, We Hear" with three letters? Next to an advertisement for Plant's Brushless Shaving Creams? *Ask him.*'

The sergeant glared at him, but spoke to the distant Stickers.

'Roc,' said Kirsty, in an absentminded way.

The captain raised an eyebrow.

'It's a mythical bird, I think,' said Yo-less, in the

same hypnotized voice. 'Spelled like "rock" but without a K. "We hear" means it sounds the same.'

'He says yes,' said the sergeant. 'He says—'

'Thank you. Tell him to be ready in case . . . no, let's not be hasty . . . just thank him.'

There was a click when the sergeant put the phone down.

Then the captain said, 'Do you know how long we've got?'

'Three minutes,' said Johnny.

'Can we get on the roof, sergeant?' said the captain.

'Dunno, but—'

'Is there some other siren in the town?'

'There's a manky old wind-up thing we used to use, but—'

'Where is it?'

'It's under the bench in the Lost Property cupboard but—'

There was a leathery noise and suddenly the captain was holding a pistol.

'You can argue with me afterwards,' he said. 'You can report me to whomever you like. But right now you can give me the keys or unlock the blasted cupboard, or I'll shoot the lock off. And I've always wanted to try that, believe me.'

'You don't *believe* these kids, do—'

'Sergeant!'

In a sudden panic, the sergeant fumbled in his pockets and trotted across the room.

'You *do* believe us?' said Kirsty.

'I'm not sure,' said the captain, as the sergeant dragged out something big and heavy. 'Thank you, sergeant. Let's get it outside. No. I'm not sure at all, young lady. But I might believe that watch. Besides . . . if I'm wrong, then all that will happen is that I'll look foolish, and I daresay the sergeant will give you all a thick ear. If I'm right then . . . this won't happen?' He waved the paper.

'I . . . think so,' said Johnny. 'I don't even know if *any* of this will happen . . . '

Bigmac was on the floor with Wobbler on top of him. Wobbler might not know how to fight, but he did know how to weigh.

'Get off!' said Bigmac, flailing around. Trying vicious street-fight punches on Wobbler was like hitting a pillow.

'I'm still alive in 1996, aren't I?' said Wobbler. ''Cos I've *been* born, right? So even if I never time travel back I ought to still be alive in 1996, right? I bet you know something about me!'

'No, no, we never met you!'

'I'm alive, then? You *do* know something, right?'

'Get off, I can't breathe!'

'Come on, tell me!'

'You're not supposed to know what's going to happen!'

'Who says? Who says?'

There was a yowl behind him. Wobbler turned his head. Bigmac looked up.

Guilty the cat stretched lazily, yawned, and

hopped down off the bags. He padded confidently alongside the mossy wall, moving in his lurching diagonal fashion, and disappeared around the building.

'Where's it going?' said Wobbler.

'How should I know? Get off'f me!'

The boys followed the cat, who didn't seem at all bothered by their presence.

He stopped at the church door and lay down with his front paws outstretched.

'First time I've seen him go away from the trolley,' said Bigmac.

And then they heard it.

Nothing.

The faint noises of the town didn't stop. There was the sound of a piano from a pub somewhere. A door opened, and there was laughter. A car went by slowly, in the distance. But suddenly the sounds were coming from *a long way off*, as if there was some sort of thick invisible wall.

'You know those bombs . . . ' said Wobbler, not taking his eyes off the cat.

'What bombs?' said Bigmac.

'The bombs Johnny's been going on about.'

'Yeah?' said Bigmac.

'Can you remember what time he said? It was pretty soon, I think.'

'Brilliant! I've never seen anywhere bombed,' said Bigmac.

Guilty started to purr, very loudly.

'Er . . . you know my sister lives in Canada,' said

Wobbler, in a worried voice.

'What about her? What's she got to do with anything?'

'Well . . . she sent me a postcard once. There's this cliff there, right, where the Indians used to drive herds of buffalo over to kill them . . . '

'Isn't geography *wonderful*.'

'Yeah, only . . . there was this Indian, right, and he wondered what the drive would look like from underneath . . . and that's why it's called Head-Bashed-In Jump. Really.'

They both turned and looked at the chapel.

'This is still here in 1996,' said Bigmac. 'I mean, it's not going to get bombed . . . '

'Yeah, but don't you think it'd be better to be sort of behind it—'

The wail of a siren rose and fell.

There were faint noises in Paradise Street. Someone must have moved a blackout curtain, because light showed for a moment. Someone else shouted, in a back garden somewhere.

'Great!' said Bigmac. 'All we need is popcorn.'

'But it's going to happen to real people!' said Wobbler, aware that real people could include him.

'No, 'cos the siren's gone off. They'll all be down their bomb shelters. That's the whole point. Anyway, it'd happen *anyway*, right? It's history, OK? It'd be like going back to 1066 and watching the Battle of . . . whatever it was. It's not often you get to see an entire pickled onion factory blow up, either.'

People were certainly moving. Wobbler could hear them in the night. A sound from this end of the street was exactly like someone walking into a tin bath in the darkness.

And then . . .

'Listen,' said Bigmac, uncertainly.

Guilty sat up and looked alert.

There was a faint droning noise in the east.

'Brilliant,' said Bigmac.

Wobbler edged towards the side of the church.

'This isn't television,' he mumbled.

The droning got closer.

'Wish I'd brought my camera,' said Bigmac.

A door opened. An avenue of yellow light spilled out into the night and a small figure dashed along it and came to a halt in the middle street.

It shouted: 'Our Ron'll get *you*!'

The drone filled the sky.

Bigmac and Wobbler started running together. They cleared the churchyard steps in one jump and pounded towards the boy, who was dancing around waving a fist at the sky.

The aircraft were right overhead.

Bigmac got to him first and lifted him off his feet. Then he skidded on the cobbles as he turned and headed back towards the church.

They were halfway there when they heard the whistling.

They were at the top of the steps when the first bomb hit the allotments.

They were jumping behind the wall when the

second and third bombs hit the pickle factory.

They were landing on the grass as the bombs marched up the street and filled the air with a noise so loud it couldn't be heard and a light so white it came right through the eyelids, and then the roar picked up the ground and shook it like a blanket.

That was the worst part, Wobbler said later. And it was hard to find the worst part because all the others were so bad. But the ground should be the ground, there, solid, dependably under you. It shouldn't drop away and then come back up and hit you so hard.

Then there was a sound like a swarm of angry bees.

And then there was just the clink of collapsing brickwork and the crackle of fires.

Wobbler raised his head, very slowly.

'Ugh,' he said.

There were no leaves on the trees behind them. And the trunks *sparkled*.

He got up very slowly, and reached out.

It was glass. Bits of glass studded the whole trunk of the tree. There were no leaves any more. Just glass.

Beside him, Bigmac got to his feet like someone in a dream.

A frying pan had hit the church door so hard that it had been driven in halfway, like a very domesticated martial arts weapon. A stone doorstep had smashed a chunk out of the brickwork.

And everywhere there was glass, crunching

underfoot like permanent hail. It glittered on the walls, reflecting the fires in the ruins. There seemed far too much to be from just a few house windows.

And then it began to rain.

First it rained vinegar.

And then it rained pickles.

There was red liquid all over Bigmac. He licked a finger and then held it up.

'Tomato sauce!'

A gherkin bounced off Wobbler's head.

Bigmac started to laugh. People can start laughing for all sorts of reasons. But sometimes they laugh because, against all expectations, they're still alive and have a mouth left to laugh with.

'You—' he tried to say, 'You— you— you want fries with that?'

It was the funniest thing Wobbler had ever heard. Right now it was the funniest thing anyone had ever said anywhere. He laughed until the tears ran down his face and mingled with the mustard pickle.

From somewhere in the shadows by the wall a small voice said, ''Ere, did anyone get any shrapnel?'

Bigmac started to laugh on top of the laugh he was already laughing, which caused a sound like a boiler trying not to burst.

'What, what, what's shrapnel anyway?' he managed to say.

'It's . . . it's . . . it's bits of bomb!'

'*You want fries with that?*' said Bigmac, and

almost collapsed with laughing.

The siren sang out again. But this time it wasn't the rising and falling wail but one long tone, which eventually died away.

'They're coming back!' said Wobbler. The laughter drained out of him as though a trapdoor had been opened.

'Nah, that's the All Clear,' said the voice by the wall. 'Don't you know nuffin'?'

Wobbler's grandfather stood up and looked down the length of what had once been Paradise Street.

'Cor!' he said, obviously impressed.

There wasn't a whole house left standing. Roofs had gone, windows had blown out. Half of the buildings had simply vanished into rubble, which spilled across the street.

Bells rang in the distance. Two fire engines skidded to a halt right outside the church. An ambulance pulled up behind them.

'You want—' Bigmac began.

'Shut up, will you?' said Wobbler.

There were fires everywhere. Big fires, little fires. The pickle factory was well alight and smelled like the biggest fish and chip shop in the world.

People were running from every direction. Some of them were pulling at the rubble. There was a lot of shouting.

'I suppose everyone . . . would've got out, right?' said Wobbler. 'They *would* have got out, wouldn't they?'

*   *   *

The siren's wail slowed to a growl and then a clicking noise, and then stopped.

Johnny felt as though his feet weren't exactly on the ground. If he were any lighter he'd float away.

'They must have got out. They had nearly a whole minute,' he said.

The sergeant had already headed toward Paradise Street. The three of them had been left with Tom and the captain, who was watching Johnny thoughtfully.

Things pattered onto the roof of the police station and bounced down into the street. Yo-less picked one up.

'Pickled onions?' he said.

They could see the flames over the rooftops.

'So . . . ' said the captain. 'You were right. A bit of an adventure, yes? And this is where I say "Well done, chums", isn't it . . . '

He walked to the yard door and shut it. Then he turned.

'I can't let you go,' he said. 'You must know that. You were with that other boy, weren't you. The one with the strange devices.'

There seemed no point in denying it.

'Yes,' said Johnny.

'I think you might know a lot of things. Things that we need. And we certainly need them. Perhaps you know that?' He sighed. 'I don't like this. You may have saved some lives tonight. But it's possible that you could save a lot more. Do you understand?'

'We won't tell you anything,' said Kirsty.

'Just name, rank and serial number, eh?' said the captain.

'Supposing we . . . did know things,' said Johnny. 'It wouldn't do you any good. And those things won't help, either. They won't make the war better, they'll just make it different. Everything happens somewhere.'

'Right now, I think we'd settle for different. We've got some very clever men,' said the captain.

'Please, captain.' It was Tom.

'Yes?'

'They didn't have to do all this, sir. I mean, they came and told us about the bombing, didn't they? And . . . I don't know how they got me down here, sir, but they did. 'S not right to put them in prison, sir.'

'Oh, not prison,' said the captain. 'A country house somewhere. Three square meals a day. And lots of people who'll want to talk to them.'

Kirsty burst into tears.

'Now, no-one's going to *hurt* you, little girl,' said the captain. He moved over and put his arm around her shaking shoulders.

Johnny and Yo-less looked at one another, and took a few steps backwards.

'It's all *right*,' said the captain. 'We just need to know some things, that's all. Things that may be going to happen.'

'Well, one thing . . . ' sobbed Kirsty, 'one

thing . . . one thing that's going to happen is . . . one thing is . . .'

'Yes?' said the captain.

Kirsty reached out and took his hand. Then her leg shot out and she pivoted, hauling on the man's arm. He somersaulted over her shoulder and landed on his back on the cobbles. Even as he tried to struggle upright she was spinning around again, and caught him full in the chest with a foot. He slumped backwards.

Kirsty straightened her hat and nodded at the others.

'Chauvinist. Honestly, it's like being back with the dinosaurs. Shall we go?' she said.

Tom backed away.

'Where do girls learn to do *that*?' he said.

'At school,' said Johnny. 'You'd be amazed.'

Kirsty reached down and took the captain's pistol.

'Oh, no,' said Yo-less. 'Not guns! You can get into real trouble with guns!'

'I happen to be the under-18 county champion,' said Kirsty, unloading the gun. 'But I'm not intending to use it. I just don't want him to get excited.' She threw the pistol behind some dustbins. 'Now, are we going, or what?'

Johnny looked around at Tom.

'Sorry about this,' he said. 'Can you, er, explain things to him when he wakes up?'

'I wouldn't know how to start! I don't know what happened myself!'

'Good,' said Kirsty firmly.

'I mean, did I run down here or not?' said Tom. 'I thought I saw the bombing but – I must've imagined it, because it didn't happen until after we got here!'

'It was probably the excitement,' said Yo-less.

'The mind plays strange tricks,' said Kirsty.

They both glared at Johnny.

'Don't look at *me*,' he said. 'I don't know anything about *anything*.'

12

Up Another Leg

What Bigmac said afterwards was that he'd never *intended* to help. It had been like watching a film until he'd seen people scrabbling at the wreckage. Then he'd stepped through the screen.

Firemen were pouring water on the flames. People were pulling at fallen timbers, or moving gingerly through each stricken house, calling out names – in a strange, polite way, in the circumstances.

'Yoo-hoo, Mr Johnson?'

'Excuse me, Mrs Density, are you there?'

'Mrs Williams? Anyone?'

And Wobbler said afterwards that he could remember three things. One was the strange metallic clinking sound bricks make as piles of them slide around. One was the smell of wet burnt wood. And one was the bed. The blast had taken off the roof and half the walls of a house but there was a double bed hanging out over the road. It even still had the sheets on it. It creaked up and down in the wind.

The two boys scrambled over the sliding rubble until they reached a back garden. Glass and bricks covered everything.

An elderly man wearing a nightshirt tucked into his trousers was standing and staring at the wreckage on his garden.

'Well, that's my potatoes gone,' he said. 'It was late frost last year, and now this.'

'Still,' said Bigmac, in a mad cheerful voice, 'you've got a nice crop of pickled cucumbers.'

'Can't abide 'em. Pickles give me wind.'

Fences had been laid flat. Sheds had been lifted up and dealt like cards across the gardens.

And, as though the All Clear had been the Last Trump, people were rising out of the ground.

'I just hope the others are still there,' said Kirsty, as they ran through the streets.

'What do *you* think?' said Yo-less.

'Sorry?'

'I mean, maybe they're sitting quietly waiting for us *or* they've got into some kind of trouble. Bets?'

Kirsty slowed down.

'Hang on a minute,' she said. 'There's something I've got to know. Johnny?'

'Yes?' he said. He'd been dreading this moment. Kirsty asked such penetrating questions.

'What did we do? Back there? I *saw* the bombs drop! And I'm a very good observer! But we got down to the police station *before* it happened! So either I'm mad – and I'm not mad – or we—'

'Ran through time,' said Yo-less.

'Look, it was just a direction,' said Johnny. 'I just saw the way to go . . . '

Kirsty rolled her eyes. 'Can you do it again?'

'I . . . don't think so. I can't remember how I did it.'

'He was probably in a state of heightened awareness,' said Yo-less. 'I've read about them.'

'What . . . drugs?' said Kirsty suspiciously.

'Me? I don't even like coffee!' said Johnny. The world had always seemed so strange in any case that he'd never dared try anything that'd make it even weirder.

'But it's an amazing talent! Think of the things you—'

Johnny shook his head. He could remember seeing the way, and he could remember the feelings, but he couldn't remember the *how*. It was as if he was looking at his memories behind thick amber glass.

'Come on,' he said, and started running again.

'But—' Kirsty began.

'I can't do it again,' said Johnny. 'It'll never be the right time again.'

Bigmac and Wobbler weren't in trouble, if only because there had been so much trouble just recently that there was, for a while, no more to get into.

'*This* is an air-raid shelter?' said Bigmac. 'I thought they were all – you know, steel and stuff. Big doors that go *hiss*. Lights flashing on and off. You know.' He heaved on one end of a shed which had smashed into the air-raid shelter belonging to

No. 9. 'Not just some corrugated iron and dirt with lettuces growing on top.'

Wobbler had rescued a shovel from the ruin of someone's greenhouse, and used it to heave bricks out of the way. The shelter door opened and a middle-aged woman staggered out.

She was wearing a floral pinny over a nightdress, and holding a goldfish bowl with two fish in it. A small girl was clinging to her skirts.

'Where's Michael?' the woman shouted. 'Where is he? Has anyone seen him? I turned my back for two seconds to grab Adolf and Stalin and he was out the door like a—'

'Kid in a green jersey?' said Wobbler. 'Got glasses? Ears like the World Cup? He's looking for shrapnel.'

'He's safe?' She sagged with relief. 'I don't know what I'd have told his mother!'

'You all right?' said Bigmac. 'I'm afraid your house is a bit . . . flatter than it was . . .'

Mrs Density looked at what was left of No. 9.

'Oh, well. Worse things happen at sea,' she said vaguely.

'Do they?' said Bigmac, mystified.

'It's just a blessing we weren't in it,' said Mrs Density.

There was a *clink* of brickwork and a fireman slid down the debris towards them.

'All right, Mrs Density?' he said. 'I reckon you're the last one. Fancy a nice cup of tea?'

'Oh, hello, Bill,' she said.

'Who're these lads, then?' said the fireman.

'We . . . were just helping out,' said Wobbler

'Were you? Oh. Right. Well, come away out of it, the pair of you. We reckon there's an un-exploded one at Number 12.' The fireman stared at Bigmac's clothes for a moment, and then shrugged. He gently took the goldfish bowl from Mrs Density and put his other arm around her shoulders.

'A nice cup of tea and a blanket,' he said. 'Just the thing, eh? Come along, luv.'

The boys watched them slide and scramble through the fallen bricks.

'You get *bombed* and they give you a cup of *tea*?' said Bigmac.

'I s'pose it's better than getting bombed and never ever getting one again,' said Wobbler. 'Anyway, there—'

'Eeeeyyyyoooooowwwwmmmm!' screamed a voice behind them.

They turned. Wobbler's grandfather was standing on a pile of bricks and looked like a small devil in the light of the fires. He was covered in soot, and was waving something through the air and making aero-plane noises.

'That looks like—' Bigmac began.

'It's a bit off 'f a bomb!' said the boy. 'Nearly the whole tail fin! I don't know *anyone* who's got nearly a whole tail fin!'

He zoomed the twisted metal through the air again.

'Er . . . kid?' said Wobbler.

The boy lowered the fin.

'You know about . . . motorbikes?' said Wobbler.

'Oh, no,' said Bigmac. 'You can't tell him anything about—'

'You just shut up!' said Wobbler. 'You've *got* a grandad!'

'Yes, but there has to be a warder there when I go an' see him.'

Wobbler looked back at the boy.

'Dangerous things, motorbikes,' he said.

'I'm going to have a big one when I grow up,' said his grandfather. 'With rockets on it, an' machine guns and everythin'. Eeeooowwmmmm!'

'Oh, I wouldn't do that if I were you,' said Wobbler, in the special dumb voice for talking to children. 'You don't want to go crashing it, do you.'

'Oh, I won't crash,' said his grandfather, confidently.

'Mrs Density's daughter's a nice little girl, isn't she,' said Wobbler desperately.

'She's all smelly and horrible. Eeeeeoowwmmm! Anyway, you're fat, mister!'

He ran down the far side of the heap. They saw his shadow darting between the firemen, and heard the occasional 'Voommmm!'

'Come on,' said Bigmac. 'Let's get back to the church. The man said they thought there was an unexploded bomb—'

'He just didn't want to listen!' said Wobbler. '*I* would've listened!'

'Yeah, sure,' said Bigmac.

'Well, I would!'

'Sure. Come on.'

'I could've helped him if only he'd listened! I know stuff! Why won't he listen? I could make life a lot easier for him!'

'All right, I believe you. Now let's go, shall we?'

They reached the church just as Johnny and the others came running up the street.

'Everyone all right?' said Kirsty. 'Why are you covered in soot, you two?'

'We've been rescuing people,' said Wobbler, proudly. 'Well, sort of.'

They looked at the wreck of Paradise Street. People were standing around in small groups, and sitting on the ruins. Some ladies in official-looking hats had set up a table with a tea urn on it. There were still a few small fires, however, and the occasional crash and tinkle as a high-altitude cocktail onion fell back to earth in a coating of ice.

Johnny stared.

'Everyone got out, Johnny,' said Wobbler, watching him carefully.

'I know.'

'The siren was just in time.'

'I know.'

Behind him, Johnny heard Kirsty say: 'I hope they get counselling?'

'We found out about that,' said Bigmac's voice. 'They get a nice cup of tea and told to cheer up because it could be worse.'

'That's *all*?'

'Well . . . there's biscuits, too.'

Johnny watched the street. The firelight almost made it look cheerful.

And his mind's eye saw the *other* street. It was here, too, happening at the same time. There were the same fires and the same piles of rubble and the same fire engines. But there were no people — except the ones carrying stretchers.

We're in a new time, he thought.

Everything you do changes everything. And every time you move in time you arrive in a time a little bit different to the one you left. What you do doesn't change *the* future, just *a* future.

There's millions of places when the bombs killed everyone in Paradise Street.

But it didn't happen here.

The ghostly images faded away as the other time veered off into its own future.

'Johnny?' said Yo-less. 'We'd better get out of here.'

'Yeah, no point in staying,' said Bigmac.

Johnny turned.

'OK,' he said.

'Are we going by trolley or are we going to . . . walk?' said Kirsty.

Johnny shook his head.

'Trolley,' he said.

It was waiting where they'd left it. But there was no sign of Guilty.

'Oh, no!' said Kirsty. 'We're *not* going to look for a cat.'

'He went to watch the bombing,' said Wobbler. 'Don't know what happened to him after that.'

Johnny gripped the handle of the trolley. The bags creaked in the darkness.

'Don't worry about the cat,' he said. 'Cats find their own way home.'

The Golden Threads Club occupied the old church on Friday mornings. Sometimes there was a folk singer, or entertainment from local schools, if this couldn't be avoided. Mainly there was tea and a chat.

This was usually about how things were worse now than they had ever been, especially those golden days when you could buy practically anything for sixpence and still have change.

There was a change in the air and five figures appeared.

The Golden Threaders watched them suspiciously, in case they broke into 'The Streets of London'. They also noted that they were under thirty years old, and therefore almost certainly criminals. For one thing, they'd apparently stolen a shopping trolley. And one of them was black.

'Er . . . ' said Johnny.

'Is this the theatre group?' said Kirsty. The others were astonished at the quick thinking. 'Oh, no, wrong church hall, very sorry.'

They edged towards the door, pushing the trolley. The Threaders watched them owlishly, tea-cups cooling in their hands.

Wobbler opened the door and ushered the others through it.

'Don't forget, one of them was black,' said Yo-less, as he stepped out. He rolled his eyes sarcastically and waved his hands in the air. 'We's goin' to de carnivaaal!'

13

Some Other Now . . .

The air outside smelled of 1996. Kirsty looked at her watch.

'Ten-thirty on Saturday morning,' she said. 'Not bad.'

'Er, your *watch* is at ten-thirty on Saturday morning,' said Johnny. 'That doesn't mean *we* are.'

'Good point.'

'But I think we are, anyway. This all looks right.'

'Looks fine to me,' said Wobbler.

'We've been out all night,' said Yo-less. 'My mum'll go spare.'

'Tell her you stopped at my place and the phone was broken,' said Wobbler.

'I don't like lying.'

'Are you going to tell her the truth?'

Yo-less thought for a few agonized seconds. 'Your phone was broken, right?'

'Yeah, and I'll tell *my* mum I was staying at your place,' said Wobbler.

'I shouldn't think my grandad's noticed I'm not in,' said Johnny. 'He always drops off in front of the telly.'

'*My* parents have a very modern outlook,' said Kirsty.

'My brother doesn't mind where I am so long as the police don't come round,' said Bigmac.

Before time travelling to any extent, Johnny thought, you should always get your alibi sorted out.

He stared at the place where Paradise Street had been. It was still the Sports Centre. That hadn't changed. But Paradise Street was still there, under-neath. Not underground. Just . . . somewhere else. Another fossil.

'Did we change anything?' said Kirsty.

'Well, *I'm* back,' said Wobbler. 'And that's good enough for me.'

'But those people are alive when they ought to've been dead—' Kirsty began, and stopped when she saw Johnny's expression. 'All right, not exactly *ought*, but you know what I mean. One of them might've invented the Z-bomb or something.'

'What's the Z-bomb?' said Bigmac.

'How should I know? It wasn't invented when we left!'

'Someone in *Paradise Street* invented a bomb?' said Johnny.

'Well, all right, not a bomb. Something else that'd change history. Any little thing. And you know we left all Bigmac's stuff in the police station?'

'Ahem.'

Yo-less removed his hat and produced a watch and a Walkman.

'The sergeant was so flustered he forgot to lock

223

the cupboard after he got the siren out,' said Yoless. 'So I nipped in.'

'Did you get the jacket?'

'Chucked it in a dustbin.'

'That was *mine*,' said Bigmac reproachfully.

'Well, maybe that's all right,' Kirsty conceded reluctantly. 'But there's bound to be some other changes. We'd better find out pretty fast.'

'We'd better have a bath, too,' said Wobbler.

'Your hands have got blood on them,' said Johnny.

Wobbler looked down vaguely.

'Oh, yeah. Well . . . we were pulling at smashed-up walls and things,' he said. 'You know . . . in case there was anyone trapped . . . '

'You should've seen him grab his grandad!' said Bigmac. 'It was *brilliant*!'

Wobbler looked proud.

They met up an hour later in the mall. The burger bar was back to the way it had always been. No-one said anything about it, but from the way he sighed occasionally it was clear that Bigmac was thinking of free burgers every week for the rest of his life.

That jogged Johnny's memory.

'Oh . . . yes,' said Johnny. 'Er. We've got this letter . . . for you . . . '

He pulled it out. It was crumpled, and covered in vinegar and sooty fingerprints.

'Er, it's for you,' he repeated. 'Someone . . . asked us to give it to you.'

'Yeah, someone,' said Yo-less.

'We don't know who he was,' said Bigmac. 'A completely mysterious person. So it's no use you asking us questions.'

Wobbler gave them a suspicious look, and ripped open the envelope.

'Go on, what's he say?' said Bigmac.

'Who?' said Wobbler.

'Y— this mysterious person,' said Bigmac.

'Dumb stuff,' said Wobbler. 'Read it yourself.'

Johnny took the paper that had been in the envelope. It contained a list, numbered from one to ten.

'"1) Eat healthy food in moderation",' he read. '"2) An hour's exercise every day is essential. 3) Invest money wisely in a mixture of—"'

'What's the point of all this junk? It's the sort of thing grandads say,' said Wobbler. 'Why'd anyone want to tell *me* that? You'd have to be some kind of loony to go around telling people that. This was one of those religious blokes that hang around in the mall, right? Huh. I thought it might be something *important*.'

Bigmac glanced at the burger bar again, and sighed deeply.

'There have been changes,' said Kirsty. 'Clark Street isn't Clark Street any more. I noticed when I went past. It's Evershott Street.'

'That's   frightening,'   said   Bigmac.

'Oooeeeoooeee . . . a street name was mysteriously changed . . . '

'I thought it was always Evershott Street,' said Yo-less.

'Me too,' said Wobbler.

'And that shop over there . . . that used to sell cards and things. Now it's a jeweller's,' said Kirsty insistently.

The boys craned around to look at it.

'It's always been a jeweller's, hasn't it?' said Wobbler. He yawned.

'Well, you're an unobservant bunch, I—' Kirsty began.

'Hold on,' said Johnny. 'How did you get all those cuts on your hands, Wobbler? You too, Bigmac.'

'Well, er, I . . . er . . . ' Wobbler's eyes glazed.

'We . . . were messing around,' said Bigmac. 'Weren't we?'

'Yeah. Messing around. Somewhere.'

'Don't you remember—?' Kirsty began.

'Forget about it,' said Johnny. 'Come on, Kirsty, we've got to go.'

'Where to?'

'Visiting time. We've got to see Mrs Tachyon.'

Kirsty waved a hand frantically at the other three.

'But they don't seem to—'

'It doesn't matter! Come on!'

'They can't just *forget*!' said Kirsty, as they hurried out of the mall. 'They can't just think: "Oh, it was all a dream"!'

'I think it's all sort of healing over,' said Johnny. 'Didn't you see it happening back in 1941? Tom didn't really believe anything that had happened. I bet by now . . . I mean, a few hours after . . . I bet they're remembering . . . I mean, they *remembered* . . . something different. He ran all the way and got there just in time. Everyone was a bit shocked because of the bombing. Something like that. People have to forget what really happened because . . . well, it *didn't* happen. Not here.'

'*We* can remember what really happened,' said Kirsty.

'Perhaps that's because you're hyper-intelligent and I'm mega-stupid,' said Johnny.

'Oh, I wouldn't say *that*,' said Kirsty. 'You're being a bit unfair.'

'Oh. Good.'

'I meant I wouldn't go so far as to say "hyper". Just "very". Why do we have to see Mrs Tachyon?'

'Someone ought to. She's a time-bag-lady,' said Johnny. 'I think it's all the same to her. Round the corner or 1933, they're all just directions to her. She goes where she likes.'

'She's mad.'

They'd reached the hospital steps. Johnny trudged up them.

She probably *is* mad, he thought. Or eccentric, anyway. I mean, if *she* went to a specialist and he showed her all those cards and ink blots she'd just nick them or something.

Yes. Eccentric. But she wouldn't do things like dropping bombs on Paradise Street. You have to be *sane* to think of things like that. She's totally round the bend. But perhaps she gets a better view from there.

It was quite a cheerful thought, in the circumstances.

Mrs Tachyon had gone. The ward sister seemed quite angry about it.

'Do you know anything about this?' she demanded.

'Us?' said Kirsty. 'We've just come in. Know about what?'

Mrs Tachyon had gone to the lavatory. She'd locked herself in. And in the end they'd had to get someone to take the lock off, in case she'd fallen down in there.

She wasn't in there at all.

They were three floors up and the window was too small even for someone as skinny as Mrs Tachyon to climb through.

'Was there any toilet paper?' said Johnny.

The sister gave him a look of deep suspicion.

'The whole roll's gone,' she said.

Johnny nodded. That sounded like Mrs Tachyon.

'*And* the headphones have vanished,' said the sister. 'Do you know about any of this? You've been visiting her.'

'That's only been because it's, you know, like a

project,' said Kirsty, defensively.

There was the sound of sensible shoes behind them. They turned out to belong to Ms Partridge the social worker.

'I've phoned the police,' she said.

'Why?' said Johnny.

'Well, she— oh, it's you. Well, she . . . needs help. Not that they *were* any help. They said she always turns up.'

Johnny sighed. Mrs Tachyon, he suspected, never *needed* help. If she wanted help she just took it. If she needed a hospital, she went where there was one. She could be anywhere now.

'Must have slipped out when no-one was looking,' said Ms Partridge.

'She couldn't,' said the sister stoutly. 'We can see the door from here. We're very careful about that sort of thing.'

'Then she must have vanished into thin air!' said Ms Partridge.

Kirsty sidled closer to Johnny while they argued and said, out of the corner of her mouth: 'Where did you leave the trolley?'

'Behind our garage,' said Johnny.

'D'you think she's taken it?'

'Yes,' said Johnny happily.

Johnny was quiet on the bus home. They'd gone to the library and he'd wangled a photocopy of the local paper for the day after the raid.

There was a picture of people looking very

cheerful in the ruins of Paradise Street. Of course, things were pretty faded now, but there was Mrs Density with her goldfish bowl, and Wobbler's grandfather with his bit of bomb and, just behind them, grinning and holding his thumb up, you could just make out Wobbler. It hadn't been a good photo to start with and it hadn't improved with age and he had soot all over his face but, if you knew it was Wobbler, you could see it was him all right.

They're all forgetting except me, he thought. I bet even if I showed them the paper they'd say, 'Oh yes, that bloke looks like Wobbler, so what?'

Because . . . they live here. They've always lived here. In a way.

When you travel in time it really happens, but it's like a little loop in a tape. You go round the loop and then carry on from where you were before. And everything that's changed turns out to be history.

'You've gone very quiet,' said Kirsty.

'I was just thinking,' said Johnny. 'I was thinking that if I showed the others this piece from the paper they'd say, oh, yeah, that looks like ole Wobbler, so what?'

Kirsty leaned across.

'Oh, yes,' she said. 'Well? It *does* look like Wobbler. So what?'

Johnny stared out of the window.

'I mean,' he said, 'it's Wobbler in the paper. Remember?'

'Remember what?'

'Well . . . yesterday?'

She wrinkled her forehead.

'Didn't we go to some sort of party?'

Johnny's heart sank.

It all settles down, he thought. That's what's so horrible about time travel. You come back to a different place. You come back to the place where you didn't go in the first place, and it's not *your* place.

Because *here* was where no-one died in Paradise Street. So here's where I didn't want to go back. So I didn't. So they didn't, either. When the newspaper picture was taken we were back there, but, now we're back here, we never went. So they don't remember because here there's nothing to remember. Here, we did something else. Hung on. Hung around.

Here I'm remembering things that never happened.

'It's your stop,' said Kirsty. 'Are you all right?'

'No,' said Johnny, and got off the bus.

It was raining heavily, but he went and checked to see if the trolley was where he'd left it. It wasn't. On the other hand, maybe it had never been there at all.

When he went up to his bedroom he could hear the rain drumming on the roof. He'd vaguely hoped that he might have been a different person in this world but there it all was: the same bedroom, the same mess, the same space shuttle on its bit of red wool. The same stuff for the project all over the table.

He sat on his bed and watched the rain for a while. He could feel the shadows in the air, hovering around the corners of the room.

He'd lost Mrs Tachyon's paper somewhere. That would have been proof. But no-one else would believe it.

He could remember it all – the rain on the moor, the thunderstorm, the sting on his whole body when they'd run through time – and it hadn't happened. Not exactly. Normal, dull, boring, everyday life had just poured right in again.

Johnny went through his pockets. If only there was something . . .

His fingers touched a piece of card . . .

The sound of Australian accents from downstairs suggested that his grandad was in. He trailed downstairs and into the little front room.

'Grandad?'

'Yes?' said his grandfather, who was watching *Cobbers*.

'You know the war—'

'Yes?'

'You know you said that before you went in the army you were a sort of aircraft spotter—'

'Got a medal for it,' said his grandfather. He picked up the remote control and switched off the set, which never usually happened. 'Showed it you, didn't I? Must've done.'

'Don't think so,' said Johnny, as diplomatically as possible. Before, his grandfather had always told him not to go on about things.

His grandfather reached down beside his chair. There was an old wickerwork sewing box there, which had belonged to Johnny's grandmother. It hadn't been used for cotton and needles for a long time, though. It was full of old newspaper cuttings, keys that didn't fit any door in the house, stamps for one half-penny in old money, and all the other stuff that accumulates in odd corners of a house that has been lived in for a long time. Finally, after much grunting, he produced a small wooden box and opened it.

'They said they never knew how I done it,' he said proudly. 'But Mr Hodder and Captain Harris spoke up for me. Oh, yes. Had to be possible, they said, otherwise I couldn't've done it, could I? The phones'd got hit by lightning and the bike wouldn't start no matter what he yelled so I had to run all the way down into the town. So they had to give it to me 'cos they spoke up.'

Johnny turned the silver medal over in his hands. There was a yellowing bit of paper with it, badly typed by someone who hadn't changed the ribbon on his typewriter for years.

'"Gallant action . . . "' he read, '" . . . ensuring the safety of the people of Blackbury . . . "'

'Some men from the Olympics came to see me after the war,' said his grandfather. 'But I told them I didn't want any.'

'How did you do it?' said Johnny.

'They said someone's watch must've been wrong,' said Grandad. 'I don't know about that. I just ran for it. 'S'all a bit of a blur now, tell you the truth . . . '

He put the medal back in the box. Beside it, held together with an elastic band, was a grubby pack of cards.

Johnny took them out and removed the band.

They had aircraft on them.

Johnny reached into his pocket and took out the five of clubs. It was a lot less worn, but there was no doubt that it was part of the pack. He slipped it under the band and put the pack back in the box.

Grandad and Johnny sat and looked at one another for a moment. There was no sound but the rain and the ticking of the mantelpiece clock.

Johnny felt the time drip around them, thick as amber . . .

Then Grandad blinked, picked up the remote control, and aimed it at the TV.

'Anyway, we've all passed a lot of water under the bridge since those days,' he said, and that was that.

The doorbell rang.

Johnny trooped out into the hall.

The bell rang again, urgently.

Johnny opened the door.

'Oh,' he said gloomily. 'Hello, Kirsty.'

Rain had plastered her hair to her head.

'I ran back from the next stop,' she said.

'Oh. Why?'

She held up a pickled onion.

'I found it in my pocket. And . . . I *remembered*. We did go back.'

'Not *back*,' said Johnny. 'It's more like *there*.' The elation rose up inside him like a big pink cloud. 'Come on in.'

'Everything. Even the pickles.'

'Good!'

'I thought I ought to tell you.'

'Right.'

'Do you think Mrs Tachyon will ever find her cat?'

Johnny nodded.

'Wherever he is,' he said.

The sergeant and the soldier picked themselves up off the ground and staggered towards the wreckage where the house had been.

'That poor old biddy! That poor old biddy!' said the sergeant.

'D'you think she might've got out in time?' said the soldier.

'That poor old biddy!'

'She was sort of close to the wall,' moaned the soldier hopefully.

'The *house* isn't there any more! What do *you* think?'

They scrambled through the damp ruins of Paradise Street.

'Oh God, there's going to be *hell* to pay for this . . .'

'You're telling me! You shouldn't've left it

unguarded! That poor old biddy!'

'D'you know how much sleep we've had this past week? Do you? And we lost Corporal Williams over in Slate! We knocked off for five minutes in the middle of the night, that's all!'

A crater lay in front of them. Something bubbled in the bottom.

'She got any relatives?' said the soldier.

'No. No-one. Been here ages. My dad says he remembers seeing her about sometimes when he was a lad,' said the sergeant.

He removed his helmet.

'Poor old biddy,' he said.

'That's what *you* think! Dinner dinner dinner dinner—'

They turned. A skinny figure, wearing an old coat over a nightdress, and a woolly hat, ran along the road, expertly steering a wire cart between the mounds of rubble.

'—dinner dinner—'

The sergeant stared at the soldier. 'How did she do that?'

'Search me!'

'—dinner dinner Batman!'

Some way away, Guilty ambled in his sideways fashion through the back streets.

He'd had an interesting morning hunting through the remains of Paradise Street, and had passed some quality time during the afternoon in the ruins of the pickle factory, where there were mice, some of them fried. It had been a good day.

Around him, Blackbury went back to sleep.

There was still a terrible smell of vinegar everywhere.

By some miracle of preservation, a large jar of pickled beetroot had been blown right across the town and landed, unbroken and unnoticed, in a civic flowerbed, from whence it had bounced into the gutter.

Guilty waited by it, washing himself.

After a while he looked up as a familiar squeaking sound came around the corner, and stopped. A hand wearing a woolly glove with the fingers cut out reached down and picked up the jar. There was a series of complicated unscrewing noises, and then a sound like . . . well, like someone eating pickled beetroot until the juice ran down their chin.

'Ah,' said a voice, and then belched. 'That's the stuff to give the troops! Bromide? That's what *you* think! Laugh? I nearly brought a tractor!'

Guilty hopped up onto the trolley.

Mrs Tachyon reached up and adjusted the headphones under her bobble hat.

She scratched at a surgical dressing. Dratted thing. She'd have to get someone to take it off her, but she knew a decent nurse over in 1917.

Then she scrabbled in her pockets and fished out the sixpence the sergeant had given her. She remembered him giving it to her. Mrs Tachyon remembered everything, and had long ago given up wondering whether the things she remembered had already happened or not. Take life as it was going to come was her motto. And if it didn't come, go and fetch it.

The past and the future were all the same, but you could get a good feed off of a sixpence, if you knew the right way to do it.

She squinted at it in the grey light of dawn.

It was a bit old and grubby, but the date was quite clear. It said: 1903.

'Tea and buns? That's what *you* think, Mr Copper!'

And she went back to 1903 and spent it on fish and chips. And still had change.

THE END

ABOUT THE AUTHOR

'One of the best and one of the funniest English authors alive' *The Independent*

Terry Pratchett needs no introduction as the best-selling writer for readers of all ages. Best known for his phenomenally successful *Discworld®* series, he is also the author of the Truckers trilogy for younger readers (*Truckers, Diggers* and *Wings*), the first of which, Truckers, was adapted into a critically acclaimed TV series. *Johnny and the Bomb* is the third title in the series about Johnny Maxwell, following *Only You Can Save Mankind* (shortlisted for the Guardian Children's Fiction Award) and *Johnny and the Dead* (shortlisted for the Carnegie Medal), which was also successfully televised.

Terry Pratchett lives in Wiltshire with his wife and daughter and says he writes for anyone old enough to understand.

JOHNNY AND THE DEAD
Terry Pratchett

Sell the cemetery? Over their dead bodies . . .

Not many people can see the dead (not many would want to). Twelve-year-old Johnny Maxwell can. And he's got bad news for them: the council want to sell the cemetery as a building site. But the dead have learned a thing or two from Johnny. They're not going to take it lying down . . . especially since it's Halloween tomorrow.

Besides, they're beginning to find that life is a lot more fun than it was when they were . . . well . . . alive. Particularly if they break a few rules . . .

'Terry Pratchett uses his wicked sense of humour to hilarious effect in his new fantasy story . . . anyone over ten can find something to smile about here' *Daily Mail*

Winner of the 1993 Writers' Guild Award
(best children's book)

Shortlisted for the Carnegie Medal

0 552 527408